P9-CPZ-146

DRAGONS in a BAG

ZETTA ELLIOTT

ILLUSTRATIONS BY GENEVA B

Random House  New York

This is a work of fiction. Names, characters, places, and incidents either are the product of the author's imagination or are used fictitiously. Any resemblance to actual persons, living or dead, events, or locales is entirely coincidental.

 Published in the United States by Random House Children's Books, a division of Penguin Random House LLC, New York.

Random House and the colophon are registered trademarks of Penguin Random House LLC.

Visit us on the Web! rhcbooks.com

Educators and librarians, for a variety of teaching tools, visit us at RHTeachersLibrarians.com

Library of Congress Cataloging-in-Publication Data
Names: Elliott, Zetta, author. | B, Geneva, illustrator.
Title: Dragons in a bag / Zetta Elliott ; illustrations by Geneva B.
Description: First edition. | New York : Random House Books for Young Readers, 2018. | Summary: In Brooklyn, nine-year-old Jax joins Ma, a strange and miserable old woman, on a quest to deliver three baby dragons to a magical world, and along the way discovers his true calling.
Identifiers: LCCN 2018015339 | ISBN 978-1-5247-7045-7 (hardback) | ISBN 978-1-5247-7046-4 (library binding) | ISBN 978-1-5247-7047-1 (ebook)
Subjects: | CYAC: African Americans—Fiction. | Magic—Fiction. | Dragons—Fiction. | Brooklyn (New York, N.Y.)—Fiction. | Fantasy. | BISAC: JUVENILE FICTION / Fantasy & Magic. | JUVENILE FICTION / Animals / Mythical. | JUVENILE FICTION / People & Places / United States / African American.
Classification: LCC PZ7.E45819 Dr 2018 | DDC [Fic]—dc23

Printed in the United States of America
10 9 8 7 6 5 4 3 2
First Edition

Random House Children's Books supports the First Amendment and celebrates the right to read.

For Marie,

whose dragons

are still

in my bag

1

Mama strokes my cheek with her finger before pressing the doorbell. I feel tears pooling behind my eyes, but I will them not to fall. Mama has enough to worry about right now.

"It's only for a little while, Jaxon. I'll be back before you know it."

I nod and look up at the peephole in the door. If I look down at my feet, the tears will fall and my nose will start to run and Mama will know I don't want her to leave me here.

Mama's biting her lip and tapping her toe nervously. She presses the doorbell again, letting it ring longer this time. We both hear someone stirring—and cursing—inside the apartment. Mama laughs nervously and says, "Ma curses like a sailor sometimes, but she's a harmless old lady. She's fun, too—you'll like her, Jax."

I never even knew I had a grandmother living in Brooklyn. Mama never mentioned her before. Sometimes Mama hides things from me—or that's what I let her believe. Mama thinks I don't know our landlord's trying to get rid of us. She takes down the eviction notices he pins to our front door, but I still know what's going on. Today Mama has to go to court. I want to go with her, but Mama wants to leave me here instead.

A heavy body shuffles toward the door. Mama and I wait patiently as at least three locks are turned. The chain stays on and lets the door open just a crack. I cringe as a raspy voice asks, "What you want?"

Mama smiles sweetly and places her palm against the door. She speaks slowly and politely. "It's just us, Ma. I called this morning and told you we were coming. Remember?"

The woman behind the door barks at Mama, "Course I remember. You called and asked if you could leave the boy with me and I said *NO*!"

The sweet smile on Mama's face doesn't budge. If anything, it hardens. Mama tries to push the door

open, but the chain's still on and my mysterious grandmother doesn't seem ready to move out of the way.

Mama puts her other hand on the doorframe and leans in so that the woman on the other side of the door can see and hear just how desperate she is. "It's only for a few hours. Please, Ma. You're all he has."

I step back and wonder if that's really true. I'm sure Vikram would let me stay at his house for a while. His parents like me and don't mind having me around. Mrs. Patel calls me a good influence. That's what the grown-ups who know me always say. But this mean lady won't even open the door and give me a chance. If she doesn't want me around, that's fine by me.

But it's not okay with Mama. She's whispering to the woman behind the door, but her smile is gone now, and there are tears shining on her cheeks. I want to hold Mama's hand, but instead I take another step back and hold on to the straps of my book bag. Mama's saying one word over and over again: *please.*

I have never seen my mother beg anyone for anything. But it doesn't work, because the door finally closes. Mama rests her forehead against it before wiping her eyes and turning to me. "Let's go, Jax," she says wearily.

I sigh with relief and take Mama's hand. Just as we

start to walk down the stairs, I hear the chain slide, and the door opens once more.

"One day. Give me your word, Alicia. *One day.*"

Mama says, "I promise, Ma." Then she pulls me back over to my grandmother's apartment. The door is open, but the lights are off and I can't see anyone inside. Mama gives me a quick hug and pushes me through the doorway. Before I can ask her when she'll be back, Mama rushes down the stairs and is gone.

2

I step inside the dark apartment.

"Lock the door, boy," my grandmother growls.

I look at the three locks on the door and decide just to flip the one closest to the knob in case I have to make a quick exit. Then I let my eyes adjust to the shadows before searching for my grandmother. The apartment smells musty, but it looks tidy. The living room has two big windows with heavy curtains that shut out the spring sunshine. I shrug off my book bag and set it down by the door. I figure if things don't work out here, I can always run away and hope the Patels will take me in.

I am standing in what must be the dining room. There's a short hallway to my right, and I think my grandmother's voice came from that direction. Light spills into the hallway, and a moment later, I hear pots and pans clanging. I figure my grandmother must be getting ready to cook something, so I move over to the kitchen and stand in the doorway.

My grandmother is wearing a purple velour housecoat that clashes with the orange-and-green wallpaper in the kitchen. The housecoat must be old because the fabric is worn thin at the elbows and around the butt area. I'm guessing my grandmother sits a lot, though I didn't see a television in the living room. Right now she's standing at the sink, peering into a cupboard that looks pretty empty.

"You hungry?" she asks in a gruff voice.

"No, ma'am," I reply.

"Boys are always hungry," she mutters before taking a jar of peanut butter off the shelf.

I watch as she grabs a knife from the dish rack and a loaf of bread from on top of the fridge. It looks like I'm getting a sandwich whether I want one or not. Her white hair shudders like an angry cloud as she smears peanut butter onto the bread, all the while mumbling to herself. I'm pretty sure she's talking *about* me, but her voice isn't quite loud enough for me to hear, so I figure she's not actually talking *to* me.

I stare at the worn patch on the back of my grandmother's housecoat and wonder what her face is like.

She hasn't looked at me yet, so I guess she's not curious about my face. I wonder if we look alike. Folks always tell me I look just like my mother. We have the same dark eyes, long eyelashes, and curly eyebrows that creep across our faces like twin caterpillars.

There's a box on the kitchen table that looks like it just came in the mail. It's about half the size of a shoebox, and lots of colorful stamps surround my grandmother's address. But there's no name written on the box—and no return address that I can see.

I go over to the table to get a better look. I slip onto one of the chairs and examine the stamps. Most of them show birds and butterflies, but others have dinosaurs and lemurs on them.

"Where did this box come from?" I ask.

My grandmother grunts and says, "Far, far away." She pauses, glances at me over her shoulder, and adds, "I have an old friend in Madagascar. You know where that is?"

I don't look up, but I can feel her eyes on me. Something tells me this is a test. Luckily, I know the answer. "It's an island off the coast of Africa," I reply.

She puts down the knife and—for the first time—turns to really look at me. I'm not sure what *she* sees, but when I look in my grandmother's face, I see an ordinary old woman who doesn't look anything like me or my mother. In fact, her eyes are a murky blue-black color, and she doesn't have any eyebrows at all. She squishes up her face and says, "Boy, what you know 'bout Africa?"

I wonder what she wants me to say. Geography is one of my specialties.

I sift through all the facts in my head and say, "Africa's a continent. There are more countries in Africa than there are states in the Union. Madagascar's in southern Africa, off the east coast of Mozambique."

She folds her arms across her chest, and her elbows nearly poke through her velour housecoat. "Well, well, well," she says in a voice that lets me know she's impressed.

I stare at the box so my grandmother won't see that I'm annoyed. People never expect a kid like me to know anything about anything. I'm used to it, but it still bothers me sometimes.

My grandmother turns back around and finishes making the sandwich. "Your mama teach you 'bout Africa?"

I shake my head but then realize my grandmother

can't see me. So I say, "No, ma'am. I taught myself." Then I add, "There are lots of rare animal species that live on Madagascar."

"Ain't that the truth!" she replies with a short laugh.

For the first time today, I start to relax. Maybe we do have something in common after all. I reach out my hand and turn the box so I can check the stamps on the other side. To my surprise, the box jumps!

My mouth falls open, but I hide my surprise when my grandmother turns around and brings the sandwich over to the table. She sets the plate down and then eases herself onto a chair.

"Eat," she says before shoving the plate closer to me.

I'm not really hungry, but I figure it's probably easier to just do as I'm told. I take half the peanut butter sandwich off the plate and keep my eye on the box. The peanut butter is thick, and it takes a long time for me to swallow just one bite. I glance over at my grandmother and see in her eyes that she's laughing at me.

"You need a beer to wash that down," she says. "Why don't you grab a bottle from the fridge?"

Beer? I'm nine years old! I figure I'll just see what's inside the fridge and pour myself a glass of milk instead. I push back my chair and take three steps across

the kitchen. I have to tug hard to open the fridge door, and the only thing inside is a head of wilting cabbage and a six-pack—of root beer.

"Want one?" I ask her.

"Sure," she says. "Why not?"

I grab two bottles and close the fridge door. That's when I notice that the box has moved from the kitchen table to the counter. I didn't hear my grandmother make a sound, but the box is definitely out of reach now.

I set one bottle of beer in front of my grandmother and watch as she twists off the cap before taking a swig.

"Ahh!" she says once she's swallowed. "Nothing like a cold beer first thing in the morning."

The clock on the wall reads 11:20, but I don't tell my grandmother that. I just sit down and open my own bottle of root beer. I take a small sip and watch the box on the counter. I think I see it move a fraction of an inch, but maybe my eyes are playing a trick on me. Maybe my grandmother just moved the box so I wouldn't get any peanut butter on it. Or maybe she doesn't want me to know what's inside.

I feel my grandmother watching me, so I look down

at my sandwich instead. I force myself to pick it up and take another bite.

"Not hungry?" she asks.

When I shake my head, she helps herself to the other half of my sandwich. With her mouth full, she asks, "You like to read, boy?"

I nod, and she continues. "Good—I got plenty of books. No TV, but you can read any book that's in this apartment."

"We don't have a TV, either," I tell her, happy to have discovered another thing we have in common.

"Oh, yeah?" she replies. "I guess your mama didn't forget everything I taught her."

I glance at the box again. This time I'm sure I see it move. My grandmother gets up suddenly and puts the lid back on the jar of peanut butter before returning it to the cupboard. She slams the door shut and says, "I need to make a phone call. When you're finished eating, just go on into the living room and find yourself a book. Understand?"

"Yes, ma'am."

"And quit calling me 'ma'am,'" she snaps. "It's getting on my nerves."

"Sorry . . . Grandma." I don't know if it's the peanut

butter or the strangeness of that word that almost makes me choke. I take a quick sip of root beer and look up to see my grandmother's shocked face staring at me.

"Boy, I ain't your granny!"

Now it's my turn to look shocked. "You—you're not?" I stammer. Did Mama run off and leave me with a total stranger?

"Well . . . what should I call you, then?" I ask.

She grunts and pushes her chair in. "What everyone else calls me—*Ma.*"

Then the woman who is *not* my grandmother shuffles out of the kitchen, leaving me alone with the mysterious box.

3

I sit by myself in the kitchen with my eyes glued to the box and my mouth glued shut by peanut butter. I try not to blink, but nothing happens for so long that I cave. Did I imagine the whole thing? Maybe there's nothing special inside that box after all.

Then I hear a scratching sound at the window, which is open just a crack. At first, I think the breeze is making the crisp, yellowed paper blind scrape against the window frame. But when the sound keeps up, I realize there's something moving out on the fire escape.

I take another swig of root beer to unglue my mouth—just in case I have to cry for help. Then I stand up and take a deep breath. I go over to the window and carefully lift one corner of the drawn blind. The sight of a furry gray squirrel makes me sigh with relief. Squirrels are harmless, but this particular one seems determined to open the window. She reaches her paws under the edge, and her sharp claws scratch against the metal frame.

"Want to come in?" I ask, even though I know she can't understand me. But to my surprise, the squirrel stops reaching under the window and nods at me!

I glance over my shoulder to make sure Ma's not around. She must have one of those really old rotary phones because I can hear her dialing it in the dining room. I tug at the blind so that it rolls up a bit. The squirrel clasps her paws together and eagerly hops from one foot to another. If I ever let a rodent into our kitchen, Mama would pitch a fit! I think they're kind of cute, but Mama says squirrels are just rats with bushy tails. I bet Ma would pitch a fit, too, but something about this squirrel makes me think it's a risk worth taking. I lift the window so the squirrel has enough room to crawl inside.

The first thing she does is hop onto the counter where Ma left the stamp-covered box. The squirrel grabs the box like she's going to lift the package up. Then she turns her head and rests it on top of the box. She closes her bright black eyes, and I realize she's listening to whatever's inside.

For several seconds, the kitchen is silent. I can hear

Ma's voice in the other room. It sounds like she's arguing with someone. Finally, the squirrel lets go of the box and bursts into a fast-flowing stream of screeches and chirps. I can't understand what she's saying, of course, which seems to frustrate the squirrel. She hops from the counter to the table and grabs what's left of my peanut butter sandwich.

"Are you hungry?" I ask. "Go on—take it. I don't want any more."

I expect the squirrel to start nibbling at the half-eaten sandwich, but instead she hops back onto the counter and sets the sandwich on top of the box. We both wait to see what will happen. A low rumbling sound comes from within, and then the box suddenly jumps and the sandwich goes flying onto the kitchen floor!

I bend down to pick it up, and that's when I feel the squirrel's four feet on my back! When I stand up, I see that she has hopped from the counter to the top of the fridge. The determined squirrel is pushing aside Ma's breadbox to reach the cupboard it's blocking.

"What's up there?" I ask. The squirrel answers in her own language and keeps tugging at the knob on the cupboard door. It seems to be stuck—or locked—and as the squirrel tries harder to open the cupboard, her feet push the metal breadbox closer and closer to the edge of the fridge. I reach up my hand to stop it from crashing to the floor before anxiously glancing over my shoulder.

"You better quiet down or Ma will hear you," I warn the squirrel.

She stops chattering and puts her front paws on her hips as she studies the closed door. Maybe the cupboard really is locked. I put my hands on my hips, too, and think for a moment. What could be so important that Ma would keep it locked away in her kitchen cupboard? And what's the connection between whatever's hidden in the cupboard and whatever's inside the box from Madagascar?

The squirrel tries to fit her claws under the edge of the door, but the cupboard still won't open. She screeches and jumps up and down in exasperation.

"Hold on—I'll help you," I say. I lift up a chair to make as little noise as possible as I move it from the table over to the fridge. I put one foot on the seat of the chair, and my second foot leaves the floor just as Ma comes back into the kitchen.

"What on earth . . . ?"

Ma's eyes dart from me to the squirrel and over to the box. I hop down from the chair and brace myself for a whole lot of hollering, but instead Ma quietly asks, "Where are the marshmallows?"

"Marshmallows?" I ask. Is *that* what Ma keeps locked away in her cupboard?

"You didn't give them any, did you, boy?" she asks with a panicked look on her face.

"No, ma'am." She glares at me, so I quickly say, "No, *Ma.*" Then I wonder just who she meant when she said *them.* Whatever's inside the box, there's more than one!

The squirrel pounds her tiny fists on the cupboard door and screeches at Ma.

"Who asked *YOU*?!" Ma cries. "You nosy little troublemaker—*GET OUT OF MY KITCHEN!*"

When the squirrel doesn't obey, Ma grabs a wooden cane that's leaning against the wall. For a moment, I think she's going to wallop me, but instead Ma raises the cane and aims for the squirrel. She jumps out of the way just in time, and Ma's cane crushes the metal breadbox instead. It clatters to the floor, and the squirrel lands on my head before hopping back onto the counter. She stands on her hind legs and chatters angrily at Ma.

"Don't you tell me how to handle my business! I may be old, but I ain't daft. Now, get—*GET!*"

Ma swings the cane again, and this time it comes down hard on the cardboard box. The squirrel and I gasp at the same time. Ma doesn't seem to care that there're things that are *alive* inside the box. She raises the cane over her head once more, but this time the squirrel surrenders. She backs away from the badly dented box, her paws held up in surrender.

Then, to my surprise, the squirrel looks straight at me. She points at the locked cupboard above the fridge before squeezing out of the open window and disappearing down the fire escape.

4

Ma slams the window shut before snatching the mashed-up box off the counter. She tucks it under her arm and spins around to face me. "I thought I told you to read a book."

I open my mouth to reply but then realize Ma doesn't expect me to say a word. My cheeks tingle with shame as I stoop to pick up the dented breadbox. I set it on the table and then shove my hands into my pockets to keep them from finding any more trouble. I open my mouth to tell Ma that I'm usually a very obedient boy, but no words come out. I almost never break the rules at home, but things feel different here. *I* feel different here. I want to ask Ma a dozen questions, but the stern look on the strange old lady's face tells me I'd better keep my questions to myself for now.

Ma prods me in the back with her cane, so I walk

out of the kitchen ahead of her and into the dark hallway. In the dining room, I see the old-fashioned phone in the center of the round table and notice there's no cord attaching it to the wall.

"Did you make your phone call?" I ask.

Ma just dumps the damaged box on the table and swats me on the butt with her cane. "Go find a book, boy," she says with a nod in the direction of the living room.

This time, I do as I'm told. I figure maybe if I don't break any more rules, Ma will tell me what's inside the box from Madagascar. I didn't notice when I first got here, but one entire wall of the living room is covered with bookshelves. Problem is, it's so dark that I can't read the titles.

"Can I open the curtains?" I ask, but Ma is busy rifling through her purse and doesn't respond. I'm relieved when the mysterious box jumps a couple of times. Whatever creatures are inside are still alive! But then Ma mashes the box with her fist, and they whimper before growing silent and still once more.

I'm so busy staring at the mangled box that I don't realize Ma is watching me. I jump when she says, "You found a book yet?"

I turn my head so that I'm facing the wall of books. "No, Ma."

"You need me to come over there and pick one for you?"

I quickly shake my head and peer at the spines of books crammed onto the shelf. Ma starts digging in her purse again, and I hear a few curse words come out of her mouth. I can't tell exactly what she's muttering, but I do hear one name over and over again: Elroy. I wonder if he's the old friend who lives in Madagascar. I wonder how Elroy would feel if he knew how Ma was treating the gift he sent.

The books on the shelf all look old and smell kind of musty. There's no dust on the shelves, but I get the feeling these books haven't been read in a mighty long time. The words on the spines are printed in faded gold ink that I can barely read. I tug open one of the heavy blue curtains so that a bit of light slips into the dark room. One thick green book immediately catches my eye: *The Wondrous Lizards of Madagascar,* by L. Roy Jenkins.

Could Ma's friend "Elroy" be this same L. Roy Jenkins?

Just as I pull the heavy book off the shelf, Ma calls out, "Come here, boy."

I check to see whether Ma's holding her cane before I take a few steps toward the dining room. Ma's actually smiling, and her cane is safely hooked over the back of one of the chairs that circle the table. It looks like she has dumped everything that used to be inside her purse onto the table. But the biggest surprise is that the stamp-covered box is open! The four cardboard flaps have been pushed back to reveal a tangle of shredded paper strips. Whatever's inside that box was packed with care. Hopefully, that means the creatures inside are safe.

When Ma sees me eyeing the box, she moves her empty old-lady purse in front of it to block my view. Then she brightens her smile and asks, "Want a mint?"

After that terrible peanut butter sandwich, I could actually use a breath mint. But I nod only so I have an excuse to go back into the dining room and get a closer look at the box. I clutch the book to my chest with one hand while holding the other out for a mint. Ma pulls a small red tin from the mess on the table. She shakes it, flips the lid open, and then dumps *all* the mints into my outstretched hand.

"Uh, I only want one," I tell her.

"Put the rest in your pocket," Ma says. "I need this tin." Then she blows the minty white dust out of the empty tin and tells me to turn around.

"Why?" I ask as I deposit more than twenty mints in my pants pocket.

"Just do as you're told, boy," Ma snarls at me. "And close your eyes!"

I take a quick glance at the open box on the table before doing as I'm told. If I want Ma to trust me, I have to follow her rules—for now, at least.

"No peeking," she warns with a sharp poke to my shoulder.

I squeeze my eyes shut and listen as Ma rummages in the box before snapping the tin shut. "Can I turn around now?" I ask.

Ma responds by shoving me in the direction of the living room. "Go read your book."

I turn around instead and try to get a look at the table. The empty box is now on the floor, and the nest of shredded paper sits atop the jumble of things Ma dumped out of her purse. The mint tin is small enough to fit in the palm of Ma's hand. What could she have put inside? I search for a reason to linger in the dining room.

"So . . . have you read this book?" I ask.

Ma doesn't even look at the book I'm holding. She starts putting things back into her purse, starting with the red mint tin. I know she just wants me to go away and be quiet, but I decide to try again.

"It looks interesting. It's by someone named L. Roy Jenkins. Do you know him?"

"Nope."

"Are you sure? His book is about Madagascar. . . ."

Ma sighs with exasperation. "Listen, boy. I never read none of those books. In fact, most of them ain't even mine. I just keep them on that big old shelf 'cause it's easier than tearing it down and putting up wallpaper."

I frown. "That's not true."

Ma stops filling up her purse and looks at me hard. "Boy, you wouldn't know the truth if it came up and bit you on the behind."

That makes my cheeks burn. What's that supposed to mean? Is this weird old lady calling me a liar? Or does she think I'm dumb? I'm not the one keeping secrets and acting shady.

"I probably know more about Madagascar than you do!" I blurt out, but Ma's not paying any attention to me anymore. She's examining a gold pocket watch that looks like it's even older than her rotary phone. When she sees me watching her, she shuts the antique watch with a sharp click and tosses it into her purse. For such a small bag, it sure seems to hold a lot of stuff.

I take a closer look at the clump of shredded paper that used to be inside the cardboard box. Mixed in with the crumpled strips are pearly purple fragments of something that looks like it's been broken. Ma tries to block my view with her body, but not before I figure out that the clump of paper isn't just packing material—it's a nest! And the purple fragments are broken eggshells. Something hatched inside that box! And the mysterious creatures must be strong to have rocked the box as they were being born. Yet they're small enough to fit inside Ma's empty mint tin.

I decide it's time to stop beating around the bush. I suck up my courage and ask, "What did you put inside that tin?"

If Ma had any eyebrows, they would have hit the ceiling. Instead, her eyes nearly pop out of her head. "Never you mind what's inside that tin!" she says in a huff. "You ain't here to get all up in my business, boy. I told your mama you could stay a little while, but that don't mean you can come in here and interrogate me."

I want Ma to trust me, but right now I'm just making her mad. "I'm not interrogating you, Ma. I just want to know what's going on. I mean, let's face it. You're acting . . . well, kind of strange!"

Ma puts her hands on her hips. "*I'm* acting strange? Who let the squirrel into the house?"

She's got me there. I look at the empty cardboard box on the floor and try to think of something else to say. Ma thinks of something first.

"Boy, you better go on and read that book before I lose my temper. Think you can come in here and mix yourself up in grown folks' business? No, sirree. You're hardheaded, just like your mama. She didn't listen to me when she had the chance, and now where is she? In court begging some judge to keep a roof over your hard heads . . ."

For the second time today, my eyes suddenly start to fill with tears. "Don't talk about my mama," I whisper at the floor, but Ma hears me just the same.

"I'll talk about whatever I wanna talk about, boy. I know your mama a whole lot better than you do. I bet you never expected to wind up here with an old lady like me, but I always knew Alicia would be back someday. She keeps on trying to outrun trouble, but life don't work that way. Trouble will come for you no matter where you try to hide. Best thing is to be ready for it. And *you* ain't ready."

I push past Ma and head for the front door, where my bag is resting on the floor.

"Where you think you're going?" she barks at me.

"Home," I say before hefting my bag onto my shoulder.

Ma tips her head back and laughs so hard her halo of hair shakes. "You ain't *got* a home—remember? That's why your mama left you here with me. Now, go sit your butt down on that sofa and read your darn book. Or throw yourself a pity party—I don't care. Just stop pestering me!"

I take a deep breath and flip the lock on the door. "No."

"What? Don't you sass me, boy."

"You don't want me here, so I might as well go."

"You're right—I *don't* want you here. But it ain't personal—it's just that I got business to take care of. So stop making a nuisance of yourself and do as you're told."

"I have friends, you know! I don't have to stay where I'm not wanted." I put my hand on the doorknob and take one last look at the empty box covered with stamps from Madagascar. "When Mama comes back, tell her I've gone to stay with Vik."

"Suit yourself," Ma says with a sigh.

Just as I turn to go, we both hear a low, menacing growl coming from inside Ma's old-lady purse. Ma scowls, grabs her cane, and whacks the bag. There's a sharp squeal, and then whatever was growling inside the tin in her bag grows quiet.

Ma pulls a chair out from the dining room table, sinks onto it, and covers her eyes with her hand. "I'm too old for this mess," she mutters.

I see my chance and take it. Before Ma can say another word, I fling open the door and dash out of the apartment.

5

I reach the bottom of the stairs before I realize that I've still got L. Roy's book tucked under my arm. I'm not sure why I brought it with me, but I know I'm not going back to that apartment! I tell myself I'll give it to Mama and let her take it back to Ma. I sure hope Mama and her lawyer win in court today. If we get evicted, we might have to move in with Ma, and I don't want to see that mean old lady ever again!

Once I reach the street, I slow down and take a moment to catch my breath. I put the heavy book inside my bag and zip it up. If I'm going to stay with the Patels, I'll need to call Vik. But I don't have a cell phone, and I don't see any pay phones on this block. I know it's unlikely that Mama will come back soon, so I drop onto the front step of a neighboring building and try to come up with a plan.

Ten minutes go by before I hear a tap-tap-tap sound on the pavement. I glance up, and sure enough, Ma is making her way toward me with her cane. She points it at me and calls out, "You—boy!"

I tell myself I don't have to look at her. And Mama always said I didn't have to respond to anyone who called me out of my name.

The tap-tap-tap sound doesn't stop, though, and soon Ma is standing before me on the sidewalk. She's wearing black leather sneakers, but I can see the hem of her purple housecoat hanging below her beige overcoat. Ma must have hurried to catch up with me. She's a little out of breath, so neither of us says anything for a minute. I look down the block, wishing I could make Mama suddenly appear. Ma looks the other way like she's waiting for someone, too.

Finally, she clears her throat and says, "I gotta make a delivery."

When I don't respond, Ma coughs lightly and asks, "You coming, boy?"

Ma isn't looking at me, but her voice isn't as harsh as it was before. Something tells me Ma's not the sort of person who's good at apologies. That's okay with me, because I'm not planning to apologize, either.

"My name's Jaxon," I say quietly.

Ma grunts and squints at me. "That your daddy's name?"

I frown. I don't want to talk about my father. So I just shrug and say, "That's *my* name, but you can call me Jax."

Ma nods and says, "Let's go, Jack."

"It's *Jax*—with an *x*."

Ma looks annoyed, but she nods again and waits for me to get up. I heave my book bag onto my shoulder, and we start walking up the block—slowly, because that's how Ma hobbles along with her cane. For a long while, we don't say a word. Then Ma clears her throat and says, "Your mama calls me Ma because I used to look after her when she was a girl. Her mother left her with me, but we ain't related. I'm just an old friend of the family."

"Why did my grandmother leave Mama with you?" I ask.

Ma stops walking and leans on her cane. She takes a few deep breaths and then looks down at me. "Raising a child is the hardest job in the world, Jax. I should know—I've raised plenty. But ain't none of 'em mine. Like a lot of women, your granny needed help. Raising a child on her own was more than she could handle, so she came to me 'cause . . . she knew I needed help, too."

"What kind of help? Like, with chores?"

"Boy, please!" Ma says impatiently.

I frown and wait for her to call me by my name. Ma rolls her eyes but tries again.

"You've seen my home, *Jax*. It was nice and tidy until you let that darn squirrel into my kitchen. I don't need anyone's help to keep a clean house. Back then, I needed a different kind of help. Another name for that kind of helper is . . . *apprentice*."

Ma pushes herself forward and starts walking once more. I want to move, but all the thoughts suddenly swirling in my head are making me dizzy. I take a deep breath and try to focus. *Apprentice.* The only time I've seen that word is when it comes after another word: *sorcerer.*

If Mama was the apprentice, does that mean Ma is a . . . ?

Then I start to wonder—is Mama really at court today? What if she doesn't come back for me? If I stay with Ma for good, does that mean I'm going to become her apprentice?

A fly nearly zooms into my open mouth, so I close it and hurry to catch up with Ma. She's squinting even though the sky is full of gloomy clouds. It was sunny just a moment ago, but I don't have time to think about the weather right now. I need to know the truth.

"So . . . Mama was your apprentice?"

Ma shakes her snowy head and says, "She could've been. Had a lot of potential, your mama. Alicia was a very bright girl—and curious, like you. But she wanted an ordinary life." Ma clears her throat before spitting a wad of phlegm into the street. "So that's what she got."

I think about that for a minute. Is getting evicted "ordinary"? It sure doesn't seem normal to me. I get the feeling Ma wishes Mama had made different decisions in her life. But if Mama had become Ma's apprentice all those years ago, would she still have met my daddy—and had me?

If I were Ma's apprentice, I'd probably already know what she's keeping inside the red mint tin. L. Roy's thick book weighs heavily in my bag, so I make an educated guess.

"Your friend in Madagascar—he sent you some lizards, didn't he?"

I hold my breath and don't exhale until Ma nods. That gives me the courage to ask another question. "And he's the same man who wrote that book, right?"

"The book you *stole*?"

"I—I—I didn't steal it!" I stammer. "I'm just borrowing it for a while." I slide one arm free and swing my backpack around so I can unzip it. "Here—I'll give it back."

Ma stops again and glares at me. "What am I gonna do with a big, heavy book out here in the street?"

She's right, of course, so I zip my bag and slip my arm back through the strap. To my surprise, Ma chuckles.

"'Sides, I done read that book half a dozen times already."

I give Ma the side-eye. "You said you hadn't read any of those books."

"And you knew I wasn't telling the truth. You're no fool, Jax. I'll give you that much."

It's not exactly a compliment, but Ma's still got something like a smile on her face, so I dare to ask another question.

"Why was that squirrel trying to give marshmallows to your lizards?"

Ma's smile disappears. She looks down the block and whistles softly. "Every living creature needs help to survive in this world, Jax. I do the best I can for the creatures in my care, but sometimes . . ."

Ma brings her milky black gaze back to my face. Then she puts her thumb on one of my creeping-caterpillar eyebrows and tries to smooth out the curly hair. Mama does that, too, and it always makes me smile because we both know our eyebrows won't ever be tamed.

"Sometimes you can't let your love show," Ma says in a soft but firm voice. "Sometimes you have to say no when you want to say yes, because it's the responsible thing to do. These drag—uh—lizards can't stay here, Jax. They came from one world, and they're on their way to another."

"Are they hungry?"

"Probably. This kind of newborn loves sweet, sticky things, but I can't give 'em what they want."

"Why not?"

"If I fed them, they'd think I was their mama. You know what *imprint* means?"

I think for a moment. Vocabulary isn't really one of my specialties, but I give it a shot anyway. "When something heavy makes an impression on something light—or soft. Like when you step in mud or wet cement and leave a footprint."

Ma nods. "That's right. In the animal world, it's a little bit different. Some animals don't know how to be—*who* to be—until they open their eyes for the first time. These little critters need to be kept in the dark until they're with their own kind. I couldn't let them see me—or you."

"Why can't they stay here? You could buy a terrarium from a pet store—and another lizard who can show them how to . . . do lizard stuff. I could help you look after them."

Ma looks up and down the block and sadly shakes her head. "Brooklyn ain't what it used to be. Sometimes I look around and hardly recognize the place. 'Artisanal' this and 'organic' that. I used to know the name of everyone in my building—and they knew mine. Now I don't even know half the folks on my floor. They move in and act like strangers, not neighbors."

Ma sighs and starts walking again. "That's the way of the world, I guess. Out with the old, in with the new. Sure is a shame, though. Brooklyn's lost its magic. All kinds of creatures used to call this place home. But not anymore."

I think about the notices our landlord keeps putting on our front door. "Everybody should have a home," I say, "and get to stay there as long as they want."

"In an ideal world, that would be true," Ma says. "But that's not the world we live in, Jax."

I feel my eyes filling with tears again, so I come up with another question. "Where are you taking the lizards? Prospect Park Zoo?"

Ma shakes her head. "These lizards are, um, special. They need a whole lot of space so they can spread their—I mean, they need room to grow. L. Roy sent them to me because he knew I wouldn't put them in a cage."

"So he *is* your friend."

Ma grunts. "L. Roy is a quack. Calls himself a scientist, but most of the time he just makes stuff up and hopes folks won't know the difference."

"But *you* know."

She nods and says with a hint of pride, "It's my job to know what's fact and what's fiction." Then Ma points her cane at the park up ahead and adds, "That's where we're going. Now, Jax—can you keep a secret? 'Cause I don't need your mama hassling me about mixing you up in my business. That's why she left home in the first place. She didn't like my line of work."

"What line of work is that?" I ask, feeling silly for thinking Ma might be a sorcerer. "Are you a veterinarian?"

"No, Jax. I'm not a vet."

"What are you, then?"

Ma looks both ways before pushing me into the empty street with her cane. I wait to see if she'll answer my question, but she doesn't respond until we reach the other side of the street. Then she turns and just stares at me for what feels like a really long time.

"Your mama really didn't tell you nothin' 'bout me?" Ma asks finally.

"No, ma'am," I say truthfully.

Ma grunts. "You got nice manners, I'll give you that," she says. Then she sighs and leans heavily on her cane—so heavily I worry it might snap in two.

"What you need to know, Jax, is . . . I'm a witch."

She says it simply, like it's no big deal. Then Ma pushes herself off her cane and hobbles over to the park.

6

We stop in front of the entrance to Prospect Park. Behind us, cars race along busy Flatbush Avenue. Joggers trot past us, and mothers push babies in strollers. Mama used to bring me here when I was little. There's a carousel and a zoo on this side of the park, plus a playground and Lefferts House, where Dutch settlers used to live. Prospect Park is one of my favorite places in Brooklyn, but being here with Ma makes me feel more nervous than excited. I put a hand over my stomach and hope I don't look as queasy as I feel. What does an old witch with baby lizards from Madagascar do in a place like Prospect Park?

Turns out we aren't actually going inside the park. Instead, we stand before the tall stone gate while Ma examines the tumultuous sky. The dark clouds above us look like water swirling down a drain.

"Looks like rain," I say, hoping that will prompt her to act. But Ma just gives me a thoughtful "hmm" before giving her bag a reassuring pat.

"What do we do now?" I ask as raindrops start to spatter my face.

"Wait," Ma replies.

I follow her over to a stone bench and watch as Ma eases herself onto it with a groan. I'm too anxious to sit, so I stand a few feet away. One or two pigeons do their jerky walk nearby, hoping we'll toss them some crumbs or something else to eat. Whenever a pigeon gets too close, I swing my foot in its direction and send it flapping away. But more and more pigeons descend from the angry sky, and soon we're surrounded by a sea of cooing birds. I stamp my foot to scare them away, but Ma says, "Leave 'em be. They know what time it is."

That makes no sense to me, but I do as I'm told and sit down next to Ma on the hard stone bench. I steal glances at her but try to act cool. I've never seen a real witch before! Ma doesn't look anything like the witches you see on TV. I want to ask her how she became a witch. Was she someone else's apprentice once? I'm curious but also a little bit scared, and I don't want to say something corny like "Where's your broomstick?" So I just crack my knuckles and wait for Ma to say something to me. She's gone back to staring at the sky, though, so nothing gets said for a while.

Before I can think of a sensible witch question to ask, a homeless man pushing an overflowing grocery cart comes our way. He's wearing so much clothing he looks like a walking pile of laundry! I count at least three different hats stacked on top of his head, which he keeps tucked in close to his chest. I can't see the man's face, but his cart carries an old TV, clear bags full of empty soda cans and bottles, and more clothes.

I try not to stare because Mama says that's rude, but Ma doesn't seem to feel that way. In fact, Ma shifts closer to me so there's more room on the bench, and sure enough, the man parks his cart and sits down right beside her.

"Ma," he says in a gruff but friendly voice.

"Ambrose," she replies politely.

I stare at the ground so no one can tell how surprised I am. Ma *knows* this guy?

"You ever think about traveling light?" she asks him. "You ought to find someplace to park that cart. It's slowing you down, Bro."

The man reaches out a gloved hand and grips the rim of his cart. "Sorry to keep you waiting, Ma, but you know I like to keep my prized possessions within reach."

Ma nods like she understands. Then she uses her cane to knock a clump of dried mud off one of his mismatched shoes. "How're things?"

The man lifts his head to gaze at the street. "Things ain't what they used to be, Ma. But you don't need me to tell you that."

"Any trouble with the transporter?"

"You traveling today?"

Ma shrugs. "Might be."

"Thought you left the game a long time ago, Ma. You ain't no spring chicken, you know!"

Ma grunts and taps her cane anxiously on the pavement. "Tell me about it. But you know how it is, Bro. Every time I get close to retirement, they find some way to keep me on the job."

Ambrose chuckles. "What is it this time?"

Ma pats her bag and says, "I gotta make a delivery."

Ambrose tilts his head to the side, which makes the fedora on top start to slide off. "That's grunt work, Ma. Why they got a pro like you making deliveries?"

Ma tugs at the straps of her bag and looks around to see if anyone's listening. "You know how it is, Bro. Some deliveries are more special than others."

Ambrose nods so hard the fedora finally does fall off. I pick it up and hand it to him—and that's when I see the gap. It's a mild spring day, but Ambrose is wrapped up from head to toe. He's wearing so much clothing I can't see an inch of his skin. But even with all his layers, I still see air between the elastic cuff of his bubble coat and his glove when Ambrose reaches out his hand to take back his hat.

Before today, I wouldn't have paid much attention to a homeless man sitting on a bench in front of Prospect Park. But now that I know Ma's a witch, nothing seems normal. If Ambrose wasn't wearing a hundred different pieces of clothing, I think he'd be invisible!

"Thanks, kid," he says before setting the fedora on top of his baseball cap. To Ma he says, "He's with you?"

Ma looks at me for a few seconds before she responds. "Yeah, he's with me."

"And the birds?"

Ma shrugs and looks up at the angry sky. "Guess they figured I needed a winged escort."

Ambrose laughs and pulls a clear plastic bag from his cart. He undoes the knot and tosses birdseed at the pigeons. They hurry over to him, clearing the sidewalk in front of Ma and me.

"First day on the job?" Ambrose asks. He keeps his head down like he's watching the birds, but I know he's talking to me.

I open my mouth to reply, but Ma beats me to it. "He's just a temp," she says.

Ambrose laughs again. "All your apprentices are temporary, Ma! Watch yourself, kid—on-the-job training in our line of work can be risky. Say, Ma, what happened to your last apprentice? Did his hair ever grow back?"

"Of course it did!" Ma puts her hand on my arm and gives me a sharp squeeze. "Don't listen to him, Jax. Bro's just messing with you." To Ambrose she says, "You ready?"

"I'm always ready, Ma. Just say the word."

Ma puts both hands on her cane and pushes herself off the bench with another groan. "Is that really necessary? We've known each other a long time, Bro."

"True. But I don't make the rules, Ma. Can't open the door until you give me the password."

Door? I look around, but the only door I can see belongs to the guardhouse. There's one at each corner of the park entrance. It looks like the tiniest castle ever built, with round stone walls and a pointed red-tiled roof. Two steps lead up to a black door that has no knob, just a gold keyhole in the center. The guardhouse used to have windows on the sides and in its door, but metal plates and black bars weave across the space where glass ought to be. It might be the perfect hide-out for rats, but why would Ma want to go in there?

The pigeons take advantage of Ma's distracted state and gather at her feet once more. Ma curses under her breath and fishes inside her purse for several seconds before pulling out a small blue book. She opens it and impatiently flips from page to page. Finally, she cries out, "Got it!"

I watch as Ma leans in close to Ambrose and whispers something in his ear. He nods and then grips his cart to steady himself as he gets to his feet. Ambrose pulls a key from a pocket inside his heavy coat and leads Ma over to the guardhouse that's closest to our bench. I hear a loud click as he unlocks the black door.

Ma waits for Ambrose to shuffle back over to his cart before she tries opening the door. Since it has no knob, she tugs at the bars over the window until the heavy door creaks open.

Ambrose deposits the key inside his coat and calls over his shoulder, "The transporter's had some irregular outcomes in the past few weeks."

Ma frowns and pulls the black door open a bit more so she can peer inside. "I don't need to hear that, Bro," she says wearily. "Not today."

"Just thought you should know, Ma, since you're taking a friend. Be prepared for potential irregularities."

"I'm always prepared," Ma says with confidence.

Ambrose nods again and pushes his cart back down Flatbush Avenue. "Well, it's been a pleasure, Ma. You take good care of yourself."

"If I don't, who will?" Ma asks with a smile.

Ambrose raises his hand, and Ma waves back even though he can't see her. Then she turns to me and says, "Ready to go?"

"Go where?" I ask as my stomach does a quick flip.

"From this world to another. Shouldn't take too long. You ever been to Coney Island, Jax?" I nod, and Ma says, "It's sort of like riding the Cyclone—bumpy, but fast."

I shoo the remaining pigeons away and walk up to the guardhouse. With all the windows blocked, it's dark inside, but enough light comes through the open door to show a second door in the back wall.

"Nothing to be afraid of," says Ma. "We just close the door, hold on, and come out the other side once we reach our destination."

"Which is . . . ?"

Ma sighs. "I know you like geography, Jax, but the place we're going to isn't on any map you've ever seen."

"And the lizards will be safe there?" I ask. I do care about them, but mostly I'm trying to delay the decision Ma wants me to make.

Ma takes the gold pocket watch from her purse. She turns it over in her palm and says more to herself than to me, "It's time."

The rain starts to fall more steadily, and people rush out of the park, paying us no mind. Only the pigeons find us fascinating. One even lands on Ma's shoulder! I would have freaked out, but Ma just strokes the bird before gently pushing it off.

Finally, Ma looks at me through the drizzle and says, "Here's the deal, Jax. The *real* deal. The creatures L. Roy sent me aren't lizards—they're dragons. There's not enough magic here to sustain these creatures. That's why they can't stay in Brooklyn."

Ma pauses to give me a chance to say something, but I'm speechless, so she goes on. "I know it's a lot to take in. I'm a witch, I've got three dragons in my bag, and I'm supposed to look after you for a while. You can come with me, but I'd understand if you wanted to go stay with your friend instead. What was his name?"

"Vik," I tell her.

"Right. You got options, Jax." Ma watches me for a moment and then says, "You look a little queasy already. Maybe you should stay with Ambrose. He hasn't gone far—if you hurry, you can catch him. I'll find you when I get back—I promise."

I peer into the dark, cramped guardhouse and wonder whether Mama was right to run away from Ma. Maybe my mother felt then the way I feel right now.

"You don't have to come," Ma tells me. "No hard feelings—really. But you have to make up your mind fast, Jax, 'cause I got to go."

A whining sound comes from Ma's purse, and more pigeons flock to the guardhouse. I glance up the block and wonder what Ambrose and I would talk about if I chose to stay behind with him instead of going who knows where with Ma. There's probably a pay phone at the nearby subway station, and the library isn't too far away. I could call Vik and tell him to meet me there.

Or . . .

I could travel to a faraway world and help Ma deliver those baby dragons.

Ma shoos the pigeons out of the guardhouse and steps inside. There's barely enough room for her to turn around. Ma smiles at me and waves before grabbing hold of the metal ring in the center of the door. "I'll be back soon, Jax," she says with a wave.

Ma is smiling, but I see something in her blue-black eyes. I think it might be disappointment. How many new recruits have walked away when Ma needed their help? I'm not her official apprentice—like she said, I'm just a temp—but I have nothing better to do right now. In my bag I've got L. Roy's book, which should teach me a thing or two about the wondrous *dragons* of Madagascar.

I already got left behind once today. I don't want to get left behind again. Just as Ma starts to pull the heavy door shut, I call out "Wait! I'm coming with you, Ma. You might need a helper," I tell her as I squeeze in.

Ma pulls the door shut with a bang. It's pitch-black inside the cramped guardhouse, but my racing heart slows down a bit when Ma puts her hands on my shoulders.

"All right, Jax—hold on. This could be a bumpy ride."

7

Ma was right—the guardhouse moves through time and space the same way the cars on the ninety-year-old Cyclone rattle along the wooden tracks. My hands reach out for something to hold, but the round walls of the guardhouse are smooth. There are no levers to pull or buttons to push. We just swerve and swoop for the longest minute of my life.

"Are we there yet?" I ask breathlessly.

"Almost," Ma says. Then she leans down and whispers in my ear, "You're doing great, Jax. We're going to land just like an airplane, so brace yourself."

When my ears pop, I grab hold of the iron ring on the inside of the back door. It feels like we're actually picking up speed!

"Hold on!" Ma shouts seconds before we plummet to the ground with a shuddering thud.

I swallow hard and take a few deep breaths.

"You okay, Jax?" Ma asks.

Her strong hands are still gripping my shoulders, keeping me upright. I open my eyes, and the sealed guardhouse is still pitch-black. My knees feel a bit wobbly, but I let go of the iron ring in the door.

I don't know if I am okay, but I'm here to help—not be helped. So I clear my throat and say, "Ready, Ma," with more confidence than I actually feel.

Ma takes her hands off my shoulders. With a grunt, she pushes open the door.

It's *hot*—that's the first thing I notice. And it's dark, even though it doesn't seem to be nighttime. Ma gently pushes me ahead of her so I'm the first one to step out of the guardhouse. My feet sink into spongy soil, and I start to sweat almost right away. It feels just like the inside of the greenhouse at the botanic garden. The plants around us look tropical. It's so humid, even the leaves are sweating! Strange squawking sounds come from the trees above. I think we're in some sort of jungle.

"Is this where dragons live?" I ask over my shoulder.

The look on Ma's face isn't reassuring. She stands in the doorway of the guardhouse and scowls at the world around us. Ma starts muttering something under her breath. I watch as she runs a finger along the dewy surface of a glossy green leaf. She sticks her finger in her mouth, pulls it out, and concludes, "Ain't no magic here."

That's not good. We left Brooklyn because there wasn't enough magic there, either. "Are you sure?" I ask. "Maybe we should ask somebody."

Ma looks at me sideways. "You see anybody 'round here, Jax?"

"No . . . but wasn't someone supposed to meet us?" I ask.

"That's usually how it works," Ma says. "I think we must have overshot the mark."

There's no gearshift inside the guardhouse, but I'm hoping Ma knows how to put it in reverse. "Let's just go back," I suggest.

Ma shakes her head. "That's the wrong direction. We need to go *across,* not back. Magic left this earth a long time ago—we won't find it in the past."

"Can you make the guardhouse go across?"

"Sure. Parallel realms exist in different dimensions. Time travel is like whizzing down a slide. Crossing dimensions is more like skipping double Dutch. You got to wait for the right moment and slip in between the ropes."

I swat at the biggest mosquito I've ever seen. My clothes are sticking to my skin, but I'll get eaten alive by bugs if I take off my shirt. "How do you steer that thing?"

"With my mind," Ma says absently.

When it becomes clear she's not going to offer further explanation, I prompt Ma to say more. "So . . . you just think about a place and that's where it goes?"

"Pretty much. Transporters respond to the intention of the traveler. I sure wasn't thinking about *this* place—were *you*?"

"No!"

Ma wipes her forehead with the back of her hand. "Whew! It's hotter here than Brooklyn in July—and twice as humid!" Ma reaches up to plump her snowy halo of hair, which is starting to droop a bit. "Well, since we're here, we might as well have a look around," she says.

I'm not sure that's such a good idea, but I trail after Ma as she pushes aside plants with leaves that are bigger than my head. She uses her cane to beat back the dense undergrowth. After a while, the vegetation thins and the ground beneath becomes rocky and hard. I'm so busy checking for snakes and other creepy-crawlies that I bump into Ma when she stops suddenly.

"Well, now. That's something you don't see every day."

I peer around Ma and gasp. We're standing at the edge of a steep cliff, and in the distance is an erupting volcano! Dark clouds of ash spew out of the top, and red lava snakes down the side of the mountain. Far below us I can see creatures fleeing from the eruption, and even from a distance, it's clear that they're dinosaurs. The distant herd of long-necked sauropods doesn't worry me, but then Ma points at something in the sky, and I look up in time to see a flock of pointy-beaked *Pteranodon* soaring overhead!

Even though they're high above us, I duck and tug at the belt on Ma's overcoat to pull her back from the edge of the cliff. "Maybe we should stay close to the guardhouse," I suggest.

Ma opens her purse. The dragons have started to screech and whine, but Ma ignores them and takes out the gold pocket watch instead. She hands me the bag and says, "Hold this for me while I check our coordinates."

I take the bag from Ma. "I thought that was a watch," I say as Ma flips open the gold case.

"It is," she says, "but it's also a compass. Hmm, that's odd."

"What's odd?" I ask anxiously.

"We seem to have gone back—way back—in time." Ma glances at the lush tropical landscape and concludes, "This must be the Mesozoic era. Jurassic or Cretaceous period, I'd say, judging from the flora and fauna. What do you think, Jax?"

"That's really not my specialty," I say, trying not to think of all the ways people get eaten in the dinosaur movies I've seen. "Why did we land here? I thought we were delivering dragons, not dinosaurs."

"There are certain similarities between the species," Ma says thoughtfully. "But you're right, Jax. This isn't our destination. I didn't intend for us to come here, but Ambrose did say the transporter was acting up. . . ."

Ma clicks the compass shut and slips it into her coat pocket. Then she squints at something beyond the edge of the cliff. She points with her cane and asks, "You see that?"

I take a small step forward and crane my neck to see what Ma's pointing at. Something is sparkling on a narrow ledge about five feet below the cliff's edge.

"Jump down and grab that for me, Jax."

I stare at Ma like she's lost her mind. But then I remember that I did sign up to be her helper, so I hand her back her purse and kneel down to get a closer look. "What is it?" I ask.

"I don't know," Ma replies, "but it could come in handy down the road."

When I hesitate, Ma adds, "The sooner you grab it, the sooner we can get back to the transporter."

I scan the red sky for more hungry *Pteranodon*. Then I take off my book bag, take a deep breath, and sit down with my legs dangling over the edge of the cliff. I check for footholds and then flip over and start lowering myself down. Ma squats at the cliff's edge, urging me to take my time, but I just want to get this over with. Last year, Vik and I got to try rock-climbing at our school. We wore harnesses in case we fell, and there were mats on the floor of the gym. I don't have a harness now, and it's a *long* way down! I focus on making one move at a time, and before long, I'm able to drop onto the ledge.

"It's just a couple of feet to your left, Jax," Ma says.

There are tufts of vegetation sprouting out of the cliff. I grab hold of a clump of grass with one hand, and with the other I reach for the sparkling shard. I tug as hard as I can without losing my balance, but the crystal doesn't come out of the cliff.

"It's stuck," I tell Ma.

She frowns and then lowers her cane so that I can grab hold of it. "Poke it with this," she suggests. "That might loosen it."

I jab the stick at the cluster a couple of times, and sure enough, part of the glittering rock comes loose. I toss the biggest shard up to Ma. She catches it and then reaches down for the cane. I tuck a smaller fragment of the rock into my pocket and start climbing back up the cliff face. It's easier going up than down, and Ma helps pull me over the edge when I'm within reach.

"Is that a diamond?" I ask once I'm back on my feet.

"Quartz," Ma says as she examines the hunk of rock.

"Is it valuable?" I ask as I slip my arms through the straps of my book bag. Before Ma can answer, the ground beneath our feet shudders as the volcano belches out more lava and smoke. My eyes grow wide, and even Ma looks worried. She slips the shard into her pocket and says, "Let's go, Jax."

Ma doesn't have to tell me twice. I take the lead and plunge back into the jungle, swatting bugs and branches out of my way. Birds in the treetops screech, and I get the feeling it's not me and Ma they're worried about. There's something else in the jungle. I can't see it, but I can sense something moving along with us. If it *is* a dinosaur, I sure hope it's a vegetarian like *Triceratops* and not a meat-eater like *T. rex*! I glance over my shoulder at Ma, but she just yells, "Keep going!"

As soon as I see the guardhouse, I dash inside and wait for Ma to join me. She pulls the door open wide but doesn't come in. Instead, Ma holds her cane before her like a sword and takes a look around. The birds are still making a lot of noise, but whatever was following us seems to have stopped. Ma backs toward the guardhouse and then steps inside. We pull the door shut and huddle together, breathing hard in the dark. We wait for the roller-coaster ride to start, but nothing happens.

I don't know what's worse—landing in the wrong place or going no place at all.

"Ma?"

"Yes, Jax?"

"Why aren't we moving?"

Ma sighs heavily. "I don't know, Jax. I better take a look. You stay here."

She shoves open the door of the guardhouse, but I grab hold of her arm. "There's something out there!"

"It's okay. I'm a witch, remember? Nobody messes

with me—I've got magic on my side." Ma pries her arm free and hands me her purse. "Hold this and be ready to go when I give the signal, okay?" Then she steps outside and pushes the door shut behind her, leaving it open just enough to let in a sliver of light.

I clutch the straps of Ma's purse and think about what I should do. I won't see any signal if I stay inside this dark guardhouse. And Ma may be a witch, but we still got lost in time, which means she needs more than magic on her side. I'm just a scared nine-year-old boy, but I came along to help Ma, so I decide that's what I'm going to do.

I set Ma's purse on the floor of the guardhouse and push open the heavy black door. What I see surprises me: Ma is sitting on a mossy log with her eyes closed. She looks calm and peaceful, like she could doze off right here in the middle of this steamy, scary jungle.

Without opening her eyes, Ma starts talking to me. "You don't need to be out here, Jax. You just sit tight, and I'll try to get us back on track in a minute or two."

"I'm your helper," I remind her. "I can't help you if I'm hiding out in the guardhouse."

Ma smiles and opens her eyes. "True," she says, patting the spot beside her on the log. "And right now I could use all the help I can get."

I walk over and sit down next to Ma. "Are you tired?" I ask her.

Ma sighs and rubs her eyes. "I been on the job too long, Jax. These old bones need an extended vacation."

"Can't you just retire?"

"Sure. But who's going to carry on? I got to think about the future of the profession—pass the torch, so to speak."

I press my lips together and think for a minute. What if Ma were to pass the torch to me? Mama didn't want to be Ma's apprentice, but maybe I could take her place.

"What about me?" I ask.

"What about you?"

"What if you pass the torch . . . to me?"

"That's sweet of you, Jax, but I don't know if you're cut out for this kind of work."

"Because I'm a boy?"

"Don't be silly!" Ma says with a frown. "I just think . . . well, Jax, you're a lot like your mama."

That's true, but maybe that could work to my advantage. "Maybe that's a good thing," I tell Ma. "After all, Mama's real smart—you said so yourself. And she's good at solving problems, too. Plus she never gives up, even when bad things happen—like when my dad died or when the landlord tried to throw us out. So maybe it's a good thing that we're so alike. I'm a quick learner, and I don't mind if things aren't ordinary all the time."

Ma's looking at me like she might actually change her mind about training me to become a witch! But then something stirs in the bushes behind us, and I jump in spite of myself. Ma puts a comforting hand on my knee.

"We'll talk about your qualifications later. Right now we need to get the transporter up and running," Ma says. "I just need a moment to clear my mind."

Ma closes her eyes again, but I keep my eyes open in case whatever's moving in the bushes is hungry and sizing me up for a snack. I want to prove to Ma that I would make a good apprentice. But I also want her to hurry up and focus on getting us out of here because I am ready to go *now.*

Whatever's lurking in the bushes behind us starts to growl. I jump up and get ready to run back to the guardhouse, but Ma doesn't budge. Instead, she just reaches her hand inside her coat pocket and clutches the shard of crystal she put there earlier.

"Tell me what else you know about Madagascar, Jax."

As scared as I am right now, I know what Ma's doing. She's trying to distract me so I won't start to panic. But it's too late for that! The leafy branches behind Ma start to wave and then snap as the creature prepares to spring from the shadows.

"Run, Ma! Run!" I cry as I sprint back to the guardhouse. I'm moving so fast that I slam into the door on the opposite side of the round stone building. But when I turn around, Ma's not behind me. She's still sitting on the log with her eyes closed!

The creature's growl builds into a full-blown roar and then—

Ma's eyes flash open. She pulls the crystal out of her pocket and holds it high above her head. Then she looks straight at me and points her cane at the guardhouse. The black door slams shut, leaving me alone in the dark.

"Ma? Ma! MA!!"

I scream and bang on the door. I lean against it with all my weight, but nothing happens. I turn around and feel along the curved stone wall until I reach the second door. I push as hard as I can, but that door doesn't budge, either. I'm trapped inside the guardhouse, which means I'm safe from the beast. But Ma's out there with only her cane and the crystal to protect her. What chance does she stand against a ferocious dinosaur?

I turn back to the door that Ma slammed shut. I press my ear against it and try to hear what's going on outside. Over the loud thudding of my racing heart,

I hear a strange crackling sound. It gets louder and louder as whatever's making the noise draws closer to the guardhouse.

"Ouch!"

I jump back as an electric shock makes my ear sizzle. I watch in amazement as blue currents of electricity snake across the doors and along the walls. Then the guardhouse starts to shake.

"MA!"

If I bang on the door, I might get electrocuted, so I just yell Ma's name as loud as I can. When no one answers, I sink to the floor of the guardhouse and bury my face in Ma's purse, even though there's no one here to see me cry.

"I just want to go home," I whisper through my sobs.

The transporter must hear me because it suddenly shoots upward and the roller-coaster ride starts all over again.

8

After a sickening loop-the-loop, the guardhouse lands with a thud and I lift my head, still clutching Ma's purse. A single blue current of electricity snakes up the door closest to me before fizzling out. I get to my feet and carefully extend a finger to test the door. No shock.

I can't tell whether the door faces the street or the park, so I just lean my shoulder against it and push as hard as I can. When the door flies open, I tumble out of the guardhouse and land on a patch of earth that's more mud than grass. I get up, brush myself off, and take a moment to look around. I'm definitely in Prospect Park, but what year is it? I sigh with relief when a jogger trots past with a smartphone strapped to her arm and wires leading up to the buds in her ears. I'm home!

Then I look at the dirt path leading into the woods and remember that I left Ma behind in the jungle. My eyes fill with tears again, but I quickly blink them away. I'm Ma's helper, and I have to find a way to bring her home, too. But I can't do it on my own. Who will help me? I pick up Ma's purse and close the guardhouse door behind me.

My heart leaps when I go around to the front of the guardhouse and find Ambrose sitting on the stone bench. Through mirrored sunglasses, he's watching the sky, which is still overcast, though it's not raining anymore. When pedestrians walk by, Ambrose ducks his head so that the airy space where his face should be disappears from view.

I hurry over to the bench but then freeze when I realize Ambrose might blame me for what happened to Ma. After all, they've been friends for a really long time. I don't think Ambrose is a witch, but what if he gets angry and refuses to help me? My heart starts beating fast, making it hard to breathe and speak at the same time. So I plant myself on the bench next to Ambrose and blurt out, "Ma's gone, Ambrose—she's gone!"

Ambrose jumps and shifts on the bench to face me. "Whoa! Slow down, kid."

I take a deep breath, but I can't calm down. "Ma's gone, Ambrose! We have to help her."

"I know Ma's gone—I sent her on her way, remember?"

I nod and then shake my head and then nod again. Finally, I take a deep breath and try to make more sense. "That's not what I mean. I went with Ma to deliver the dragons, but something happened to the transporter. It took us back in time—*way* back—instead of crossing to another dimension. When we landed, there was no magic, but there were plenty of dinosaurs. One attacked us, and that's when I—I . . ." My voice dwindles to a whisper, and Ambrose has to lean in to hear me confess, "I left Ma behind."

For a while, Ambrose doesn't say a word. I see my reflection in the mirrored lenses of his sunglasses. I look as scared and guilty as I feel.

Ambrose finally raises his gloved hand to scratch the place where his chin should be. "Hmm," he says thoughtfully. "Sounds like you need a guide—someone to steer the ship, so to speak. And it has to be someone who can navigate between dimensions."

"Another witch?" I ask hopefully.

"Not quite," says Ambrose. "But he's the best man for the job. He's the *only* man for the job, really, so let's hope he's in town. You say there were dinosaurs in this other place?"

I nod and glance at the harmless pigeons strutting along the sidewalk. It's hard to believe that today's birds are the last of the dinosaurs. "We were in a jungle, and there was an erupting volcano . . . and I climbed down a cliff to get Ma this sparkling stone—quartz, she called it."

Even though he has no face, somehow I know that Ambrose is smiling. "Ah, quartz," he says. "That changes everything." Ambrose points at Ma's purse and asks, "What else did she have on her when you . . . uh, got separated?"

I think for a moment. "She had her cane. And her pocket watch—that was in her coat pocket."

"Not fully armed, but well equipped," Ambrose says. Then he asks, "You know any dinosaur experts?"

I nod eagerly. "My friend Vik knows a lot about dinosaurs—more than anyone I know!"

Ambrose sifts through his many pockets before producing two sleek silver phones. "Here," he says as he offers one to me. "You call your people and I'll call mine. That's how we're going to fix this, Jax—teamwork."

I take the phone from Ambrose. It's not locked, so

I go ahead and tap out Vik's number. The phone rings several times before Vik's little sister, Kavita, picks up.

"Is Vik there?" I ask her. "This is Jaxon. I have to talk to him right away!"

"Just a moment, please," Kavita says softly.

It feels like forever, but only a few seconds pass before Vik picks up the phone.

"Hey, Jax," he says in his usual friendly voice. "What's up?"

Out of habit I say, "Not much." Then I remember that there's a *lot* going on right now. I'm just not sure where or how to begin.

Vik makes it easy for me. "Where are you?" he asks. "It sounds kind of loud."

Whoever's on the other end of Ambrose's call must have a good sense of humor because he's got Ambrose cracking up. I move a few feet away and say, "I'm at Prospect Park, Vik. Can you come out? I really need your help. Like, *now.*"

Vik doesn't say anything, and for a moment I worry he's going to turn me down. Then I realize Vik's got his hand over the phone so I can't hear the conversation he's having with someone else.

"I could probably sneak out before dinner, but my

little sister says she'll tell on me unless I bring her along. Is that okay?"

What we need right now is a grown-up, not a little kid. But Ambrose is still laughing into his phone, so that must mean he's got another adult lined up to take Ma's place.

"Sure, Vik, no problem. Can you come right away? I'm at the entrance on Flatbush—across from the botanic garden."

"I know the one," Vik assures me. "Be there in fifteen minutes, Jax."

"Thanks, Vik! You're a lifesaver."

I hang up and think about what I just said. *Lifesaver.* I don't know if Ma's life needs saving, or what a couple of kids could even do to help her right now. But another burst of laughter from Ambrose gives me hope. He holds the phone to his ear even though it's covered by the red toque pulled over his invisible head. Two baseball caps are stacked on top of the toque, and the fedora wobbles at the top as Ambrose laughs.

"Thanks, man. I got to go, but I'll tell the kid to wait for you here. What's that? You can't miss him, Trub—he's got your crazy eyebrows!"

Ambrose laughs again and ends the call before slipping the phone back into his pocket. I hand him the second phone, and he puts it in another pocket before leaning back on the bench.

"Whew! I think we're set, kid. I called in a favor from an old friend. Name's Trub—and he can't *wait* to meet you."

"Why—is he mad at me?" I ask nervously.

"Mad? Course not! Matter of fact, Trub's a not-so-distant relation of yours, kid. He'll be happy to see you."

There are lots of things I want to ask about Trub, but I settle on the most important question: "Will he know how to find Ma?" I ask.

Ambrose nods and manages to catch his fedora before it topples off his head. "If she wants to be found, Trub will find a way to reach her."

"*Wants* to be found? What do you mean? She's not hiding from us, Ambrose—I left her behind!"

Tears spring to my eyes, but I manage to stop them from trickling down my cheeks. I can't stop my nose from running, though, so I open Ma's purse and fish around for her packet of tissues. Ambrose uses one of his gloved hands to pat me on the back.

"Don't be so sure—and don't be so hard on yourself, kid. The transporter misfires now and again, but Ma don't make mistakes. Could be this is all part of her plan."

"Plan? How could she plan to send me back alone? There were dinosaurs, Ambrose—real dinosaurs! Ma wouldn't *choose* to stay behind in a place like that—would she?"

Ambrose shrugs. "Hard to say. But if Ma thought you could do something on your own, she might have sent you back so she could deal with other matters."

I think about that for a moment. Maybe Ma sent me back alone because she trusted me. I do have the dragons, after all, and keeping them safe is a big responsibility. "But . . . I was supposed to help her," I say meekly.

Ambrose chuckles again. "You're helping her now, kid. I'm glad Ma's got such a loyal assistant. It's hard to find good help these days." Ambrose heaves himself to his feet. "Listen—I got to shove off, but Trouble's on his way. You sit tight, and he'll make everything right. Just you wait and see."

The man I'm waiting for is called Trouble? I feel like I've had as much trouble as I can handle for one day. But I still thank Ambrose for his help and wave as he pushes his cart away. I hold Ma's purse on my lap and hope that Vik gets here soon. I'm not sure how to tell him about Ma, so I practice telling my story in my head until I see Vik coming up the block, holding his sister's hand.

I set Ma's bag down on the bench and stand up to wave at Vik. His sister has her nose buried in a book, but I still say hi once she's close enough to hear me. Kavita barely glances at me before slipping off her book bag and taking a seat next to Ma's purse on the bench. I recognize Kavita's book bag because Vik had the same one a couple of years ago. It has green plates on it to mimic the spine of a dinosaur. I didn't know Kavita was also into dinosaurs, but two experts are better than one.

"What's with the bag?" Vik asks with a smirk on his face.

I'm so busy thinking about Kavita's book bag that it takes a second for me to realize Vik's talking about Ma's purse. "It's not mine," I tell him. "It belongs to—uh, a friend of mine."

"And she asked you to hold her purse?" Vik asks suspiciously as he looks around for my mystery friend.

"Not exactly," I reply. "This is going to sound crazy, Vik, but I swear everything I'm about to tell you is true!"

Vik just laughs and says, "Strange things happen all

the time on my block. *I* could tell *you* some stuff you'd find hard to believe."

"Like what?" I ask skeptically.

Vik glances at his little sister, but she seems absorbed in her book. "You know Carlos and Tariq, right?"

"Sure—they're in Mr. Benson's class," I say.

"Right. Well, a few months ago, they were fixing up the backyard of this run-down house on Barkley Street and they found . . . a phoenix!"

"No way!"

"It's true!" Vik insists. "We found a picture of it in the Brooklyn Museum. We tried to take care of it, but it was nearing the end of its life, so . . ." Vik looks over at his sister and decides not to finish his sentence.

But I need to know the fate of the phoenix. "So what happened?" I ask him.

Vik leans in and says, "It went up in flames! But that means a new phoenix was born from the ashes. I haven't seen it yet, but I keep my eyes open just in case. You never know what you might find in Brooklyn!"

I don't know what to say. Ma said magic was leaving the city, but maybe she was wrong. Or maybe Ma was right, and Vik's baby phoenix had to find somewhere else to live. The best part of Vik's story is that I've never heard it before—which means he knows how to keep a secret!

"So," Vik says, "what's *your* unbelievable story?"

I make sure Kavita is still engrossed in her book. Then I step closer to Vik and say, "My friend's missing and . . . she's a witch."

Vik doesn't blink, so I go on. "She received an important package from Madagascar and instructions to take good care of what was inside."

"And what was inside?" Vik asks.

"Three dragons."

This time Vik's eyes grow wide. "*Actual* dragons?"

I nod but then confess, "Well, I haven't seen them—but that's what Ma said."

"She saw them?"

"Uh, not exactly. Ma kept them in the dark because there's this thing called imprinting. . . ."

Vik nods like he doesn't need an explanation. "And your friend didn't want the dragons to get attached to a human. Smart move. So where are the dragons now?"

I point at Ma's bag over on the bench. Then my heart skips a beat. The first thing I notice is that Kavita is no longer reading her book. The second thing I notice is that the familiar red mint tin is on her lap—and it's open!

"NO!" I cry, but it's too late. Not only are three tiny dragons peering out of the tin—Kavita is *feeding* them.

"Kavi! What are you doing?" Vik asks.

"Sharing my snack," she replies without even looking at her brother.

Vik and I draw closer to get a better look at the dragons. They're so tiny that they must have had plenty of room inside Ma's mint tin. Two have wings, and one has a long body with plates along its curved spine. All of them have purply scales that shimmer like the feathers that circle the necks of the strutting pigeons. The dragons look harmless, and they purr happily as they eat the crumbs Kavita is sharing with them.

I point at the plastic sandwich bag on Kavita's lap. Inside are two round ivory-colored cakes. One is whole, and the other has been broken into pieces by Kavita so that she can feed the hungry dragons.

I remember what Ma said about not giving the dragons marshmallows. "What's in the bag?" I ask anxiously.

"That's peda," Vik explains. "My aunty brought us some from her shop in Queens."

I've never heard of peda, but the dragons can't get

enough of it. Kavita laughs as they nip at her fingers and jostle for more.

"Ma said newborn dragons love sticky, sweet things," I tell Vik.

"Then they'll love peda," he says. "It's made from milk, sugar, and cardamom."

Vik reaches into his sister's bag and takes out the cake that's still whole. A sliced green pistachio nut has been pressed into its center. Vik breaks the cake and hands half to me. "Try it."

Vik pops his half of the peda into his mouth. I take a small bite at first but quickly cram the rest in my mouth, too. It's so good! For a moment, none of us say a word as we savor the sweet, creamy cake. But as the sugary treat dissolves, I realize we have an even bigger problem now. The dragons are gazing up at Kavita with adoration. And I could be wrong, but it looks like they're a little bit bigger than they were just five minutes ago.

I don't want to go off on a little girl, so I start with a simple question. "Hey, Kavi—how did you find the dragons?" I ask.

"I needed a napkin, so I looked in your purse—"

"It's not *my* purse," I tell her. "It belongs to Ma."

Kavi rolls her eyes and says, "Whatever. I was looking in your *mom's* purse when I heard something crying, so I—"

"Dragons don't cry," Vik says irritably.

"How do you know?" Kavita asks in a voice that

sounds just as annoyed. "They sounded sad, so I opened the tin and gave them some of my snack."

I look at Vik, and he looks at me before sighing heavily. I'm guessing this isn't the first time his little sister has caused so much trouble.

She might be faking it, but Kavita gives us an innocent look and asks, "What's the big deal?"

"You had no right to poke around in Jaxon's purse!" Vik says angrily.

"It's *not* my purse," I remind him.

"That's right—it belongs to a *witch*!" Vik hisses that last word, and Kavita's eyes grow wide. "But *you* meddled with her dragons, and now they think *you* are their mother," Vik tells her.

"I don't mind," Kavita says while stroking the wingless dragon under its chin. The two winged dragons get jealous and clamor for her attention, rubbing against her arm like cats.

"*I* mind!" I exclaim. Then I look around at the people going in and out of the park and realize I need to keep it down. "Those dragons aren't supposed to be here," I tell Kavi. "They were supposed to be delivered to someone else, but now you've ruined everything!"

If Kavita feels bad about what she's done, she sure

doesn't show it. Vik picks up the red tin and holds it in his palm. "Put them back in, Kavi—now," he demands.

Kavita frowns. "They don't want to stay inside that horrible little tin."

"It doesn't matter what they want!" I cry. "They need to stay hidden until we can find Ma and deliver them to the right dimension."

"Just put them back, Kavi, or I'll tell Mummy you were going through a stranger's bag."

That works. Kavi puts all three dragons in her palm and lifts them to her mouth to give each one a kiss. Then she sets them in the tin one by one. But when Vik tries to close the lid, the dragons screech and howl like they're in pain.

I snatch the tin from Vik and try to force it shut.

"Stop—you're hurting them!" Kavita cries.

Vik sighs and says to me, "I think you're going to need a bigger tin, Jax."

He's right. Just a few crumbs of peda have led to a dragon growth spurt. We're going to need a larger container.

"What about the plastic bag?" I ask. "Let's put them in there for now and zip it up."

Vik grabs the bag with the leftover peda from his sister's lap. He takes out the crumbling cake and offers it to me. I shove the peda in my mouth and then dump all three dragons from the tin into the little bag. But as soon as they start eating the crumbs sticking to the bottom of the bag, their scaly, writhing bodies start to grow some more.

"Ouch!" Vik cries before dropping the bag on the ground.

I snatch it up from the ground and see that one corner of the plastic bag has melted.

"Uh-oh," I say. "I think these are fire-breathing dragons!"

I unzip the bag and a wisp of smoke rises from the mouth of the wingless dragon.

"We need something fireproof," Vik suggests. "I might have something at home. . . ."

I shake my head and watch the dragons as they flick their forked pink tongues over the few peda crumbs left in the plastic bag. "I don't have time. Trouble's on his way."

Vik gives me a funny look. "Trouble?"

"That's Ma's replacement," I tell him. "You and your sister don't have to stay, Vik. I honestly don't know what's going to happen next."

Vik puts a reassuring hand on my shoulder and says, "Well, we'll wait with you and find out."

"What will you do with the dragons?" Kavita asks as she gets up from the bench.

"That's up to Jaxon, not you," Vik snaps at his sister. "You need to learn to mind your own business, Kavi."

Kavi turns away in a huff and unzips her own bag to place her book inside. I take up Ma's purse and search inside for another container. When I can't find a suitable replacement for the mint tin, I unzip a side pocket and put the sandwich bag inside. Then I close the side pocket and click the latch that holds Ma's purse closed.

"Sorry about my sister," Vik says. "I should have kept a closer eye on her."

I turn around and shrug wearily. "Don't worry about it, Vik. It's been a crazy kind of day," I tell him. I look up the block and see a tall man with a bushy gray beard and furry gray eyebrows coming our way. "And it's not over yet."

The tall man holds out his hand before he reaches us. But with three long strides, he's standing right in front of me.

"You must be Jax," he says with a big smile that reveals a gold tooth. "I'm Charlie Randall, but my friends call me Trub."

9

"Who do have we here?" Trub asks. I notice that his eyes gleam along with his gold tooth whenever he smiles.

"This is my friend Vik and his sister, Kavita."

Trub shakes both their hands and then points to the bench and says, "Why don't we sit down? I can think on my feet, but we can make a better plan if we put our heads together."

I sit down first. Trub sits on one side of me, and Vik sits on the other. Kavita holds Ma's purse on her lap and sits at the far end of the bench. I notice she leaves a lot of space between herself and her brother.

"So," Trub says as he rubs his hands together, "what can I do for you, Jax?"

I know it's rude to stare, but I can't stop looking at Trub's bushy eyebrows. The gray and white hairs far outnumber the black ones, but there's no denying his eyebrows look a lot like mine. I want to ask him how we're related, but first I need to answer his question.

"Ambrose said you could navigate between dimensions. Ma tried to do it, but something went wrong with the transporter." I point to the guardhouse behind us, and Trub nods like he understands.

"What's a transporter?" asks Kavi, but Vik shushes his sister.

"Mind your business, Kavi."

She sulks and turns away from us while I finish telling my story to Trub. Vik listens closely but doesn't say a word. When I reach the end, Trub strokes his bushy beard and thinks for a moment.

"So there are two things we have to do: deliver the dragons and find Ma. Which one do you want to do first?"

"Find Ma," I say without hesitation. "When I left her, she was in trouble."

"Ma's got a nose for trouble," he says with a chuckle. "That's how she found me! Of course, there are different kinds of trouble. What's Ma up against this time?"

"A dinosaur, I think."

Vik grabs my arm. "A real dinosaur?"

I understand Vik's excitement, but this isn't a story

I'm proud to share. "Well, there was something moving in the jungle—following us. And then just as it was about to attack . . . Ma sent me back. Alone."

"I don't suppose you two figured out where you were in time," Trub says doubtfully.

I think back to what Ma said when she checked her compass. "Ma thought it was the Mesozoic era."

"Triassic period?" Vik asks.

"Jurassic, maybe."

"What kind of creatures did you see?" Trub asks.

"I wasn't trying to get up close and personal with anything in that world, but . . . there were *Pteranodon* flying in the sky!" I tell him.

"They lived from the late Triassic to the Cretaceous period, though technically they're not dinosaurs," Kavita says in a know-it-all sort of way.

"They're flying lizards," Vik explains.

"Lizards?" I think for a moment and then slip off my book bag. I pull out L. Roy's massive book and show it to Trub. "Ma loaned me this. And the man who wrote it is the one who sent the dragons from Madagascar."

Trub takes the book from me and opens it up. "L. Roy Jenkins. I haven't heard that name in a while. Thought he was in Australia, not Africa."

Vik checks his watch and stands up. "I wish I could stick around, Jax, but it's almost time for dinner. I think we'd better head home. Is there anything else you need?"

"Just one more thing, Vik. How long did *Pteranodon* stick around before they went extinct?"

"Over a hundred million years," Kavita replies, even though I wasn't asking her. "Anything else?"

I check with Trub, who shakes his head. "Thanks for coming out, Vik," I say.

"Anytime, Jax," he replies. "I hope you find your . . . Ma. Let's go, Kavita."

Vik's little sister gets up from the bench and reluctantly hands over Ma's purse. Vik nudges her and says, "Kavita wants to tell you something, Jax."

I look at her for a long time, but she doesn't say a word. Vik nudges her again, harder this time. Kavita sighs and looks at her shoes. "I'm sorry about what happened before," she says quietly.

I feel kind of bad for yelling at her, so I say, "Don't worry about it. And thanks for sharing your snack—with all of us!"

Kavita smiles at me and then takes her brother's hand. I watch as they walk down the block, the fabric plates on Kavita's dinosaur bag flapping in the breeze.

I figure Trouble and I will get back into the transporter, but he surprises me by asking, "You hungry?"

I haven't had anything to eat since choking down that peanut butter sandwich that Ma made for me this morning. I want to say yes, but it feels wrong to put my stomach ahead of Ma.

"Yeah, but . . . shouldn't we get back to Ma?" I ask uneasily.

Trouble puts his hand on my shoulder and looks me square in the eye. "Ma's gonna be all right, son. I know this business is new and strange to you, but I been doing it off and on for twenty years. And if there's one thing I know for sure, it's that Ma can take care of herself."

I think back to the moment in the jungle when Ma pointed her cane at the guardhouse. Before the door closed, Ma's eyes had locked on mine. Even with the wild creature charging toward her, Ma didn't looked afraid. "Ambrose thinks Ma sent me back on purpose," I tell Trub.

"Course she did," he replies. "Ma ain't perfect, but she also don't make no mistakes, if you know what I mean."

I didn't, but I nodded anyway, and Trub went on.

"Could be she sent you back for a reason—maybe

to meet me!" Trub laughs, and his gold tooth catches the sun, which is finally starting to come out. "One thing I know for sure is, we can't work on an empty stomach. Let's grab a burger to go," Trouble says. "We can even eat on the way, if you like."

I imagine myself trying to eat while swooping and swerving inside the transporter. Then I picture myself puking all over Trub in the cramped guardhouse.

"Maybe we should eat first," I suggest.

Trouble nods and steers me up the block with his hand still on my shoulder. Mama doesn't usually let me eat fast food, but there's a burger joint right across the street, and that's where we're heading. I walk alongside Trub, wanting to ask a dozen questions but not knowing where to start.

"Ambrose says we're related," I say shyly as we wait for the light to change.

"That's right," Trouble says with his gold-toothed smile. "I've wanted to do this for years."

"Do what?" I ask.

"Take my grandson out for a burger!"

The light changes, but I don't step off the curb. Instead, I turn to take a closer look at Trub. There's definitely a strong resemblance, but if he really is my grandfather, why hasn't Mama ever mentioned him to me? After my daddy died, Mama made it seem like it was just the two of us against the world. And I liked it that way because I knew I could count on her to be there for me. I always figured Mama was such a good mother because her own parents weren't there for her when she was my age. If she couldn't count on her father back then, why should I trust him now?

Trub watches me as if he can see all the questions swirling in my mind. He smiles and gives my shoulder another squeeze. "I sure am glad to see you, son, though I wish we could have met under different circumstances. You probably got a lot of questions for me, so how about we get some grub and then start catching up?"

That sounds like a reasonable plan, so I save my questions until we're back on the stone bench in front of the guardhouse, eating greasy burgers and fries.

"So . . . where have you been? I mean, Mama never told me I had a grandfather living in Brooklyn."

Trub takes a long sip of soda and then rattles the ice left in his cup. "Well, I can't say I blame her. I been in and out of the city for the past twenty years. A rolling stone, if you know what I mean."

I don't, but I solve the riddle myself instead of asking Trub for an explanation. Stones don't usually roll, so I figure Trub must mean that he wasn't around much when Mama was young. I pretty much knew that already, so I move on to my next question. "Are you, like, a witch? Or a warlock?"

Trub shakes his head and brushes crumbs out of his beard. "I ain't had no particular kind of training—nothing formal, at least. And no training means no title. But that don't bother me. I just help out whenever and wherever I can. Ma, she calls me Trouble Man—or Trub for short."

"Is that 'cause you get into trouble a lot?" I ask.

Trub doesn't answer right away. He balls up the foil wrapper from his burger and stuffs it inside the grease-stained paper bag that's between us on the bench. "Well, Jax," he finally says, "sometimes I find trouble . . . and sometimes trouble finds me."

I expect Trub to smile or wink at me like he usually does, but this time my grandfather just sighs.

"There's a song by the same name—don't suppose you've heard it. It came out long before your time."

"How's it go?" I ask.

Trub crumples up the bag of trash and aims for the garbage can a few feet away. He makes the shot, but Trub still doesn't smile. "It's by a great musician named Marvin Gaye. He was very talented but also very troubled. In his song, he says, 'There's only three things that's for sure: taxes, death, and trouble.'"

I suck the last of my soda through the straw. Then I burp and say, "That sounds like a really depressing song."

Trub smiles. "It's got a good beat. You like jazz?"

I shrug. I think my daddy used to listen to jazz records, but Mama doesn't play them anymore.

Trub says, "One of these days I'll play that song for you. It might sound depressing, but really it's about not letting life get you down."

I nod and gather up what's left of my meal. My aim's not that great, so I carry it over to the trash can, but before I get there, the biggest rat I've ever seen scurries across my path. I holler and jump back. The rat's heading straight for Trub, but he doesn't seem concerned. In fact, he pats the spot where I was sitting on the bench and grins when the rat hops up and puts its front paws on his leg!

There are plenty of rats in Brooklyn. They're dirty and nasty and carry disease (remember the Plague?), so I definitely keep my distance. I'm expecting this giant rat to take a big bite out of my grandfather's leg, but instead he asks, "Hey, Trub—got any grub?"

“You’re too late, Nate. Grub’s gone. Where you been?”

The rat puts one paw on his hip and looks like he’s ready to tell Trub a long story, until he sees me—or rather, the uneaten food in my hands.

“Hey, kid,” the rat calls out. “You gonna eat that?”

I shake my head and set my leftovers on the ground. I barely have time to pull my hand away before Nate hops off the bench and starts devouring my cold fries. When a hungry pigeon tries to steal a bit of hamburger bun smeared with ketchup, Nate rushes at the poor bird and sends it squawking.

I slip back onto the bench and ask, "Friend of yours?"

Trub nods and says, "Me and Nate go way back. He's no ordinary rat."

I watch the rat greedily gobbling down my leftovers and try to see what makes Nate so special. Trub can tell I'm not impressed.

"Nate's got a nose like no other," he explains. "All rats can sniff out food, but Nate—" Trub pauses to beam at his rodent friend. "Nate's got a nose for magic."

"Magic has a smell?"

Nate stops eating and looks at me over his shoulder. "Everything has a smell, kid. Magic, joy, fear, regret—all of it can be detected if you've got the right nose." He taps his snout with one claw before rising up on his haunches to sniff the air.

"What do you smell, Nate?" Trub asks.

The rat turns away from us and sniffs again. "Strange. . . . There's a trace of envy in the air. And something else . . ." Nate sniffs again and then looks at us. "I smell a thief!" he says in a grave voice.

I tighten my hold on Ma's purse and glance around nervously.

Trub frowns. "Close by?" he asks.

Nate shakes his head and strokes his whiskers. "Long gone." Then he grins and rubs his paws together. "But I do love a challenge! Gotta run, Trub. Thanks for dinner, kid."

Nate scurries over to the curb and disappears inside the sewer. "Can he really smell a thief down there?" I ask Trub.

He nods and gets to his feet. I pick up my trash off the ground and place it in the can. When I turn around, Trub surprises me by saying, "When Nate said he could smell regret, he was talking about me."

"What do you regret?" I ask.

"So many things," Trub says, slowly shaking his head. "I sure was sorry to hear about your daddy, Jax."

My cheeks start to burn, and suddenly, I want nothing more than to be squeezed inside the dark guardhouse, hurtling through time. I stand before Trub with my eyes glued to the ground. He reaches out a hand and gently runs his thumb along my eyebrows the way Mama does sometimes. I look at my grandfather and ask, “How did you find out?”

“I may not be around all the time, but I’ve always kept tabs on you and your mama.”

“You weren’t at the funeral,” I say softly, hoping to hide the accusation in my heart.

“I *was* there, but . . . I thought it was best for me to keep a low profile. A funeral isn’t really the right time for a family reunion. And the last time we talked, your mama made it clear that she didn’t want me interfering in her life.”

“Mama said that?”

Trub nods. “That was over ten years ago—before you were born. Can’t say I blame her. You see, I couldn’t always find steady work when your mama was a little girl. And that meant she had to go without some things sometimes. Plus, I had some buddies who were kind of shady, and I got mixed up in some of their mess. But when Ma introduced me to the realm of magic . . . everything changed. For the first time in my life, I really felt like I belonged—I was useful again! Ma believed in me, and that made it easy to believe in myself. I thought I could just wrap that world up in a rainbow and give to Alicia. But she didn’t want no part of it—or me, after that.”

"If you knew Mama didn't like magic, why did you leave her with Ma?"

"I didn't. But my wife—your granny—she got the wrong end of the stick when it came to me and Ma. And so she dropped Alicia right in the middle of it. Some folks fear magic, Jax—black magic especially. But in the other realm, there is no black or white. There's less fear and more . . . wonder." Trub smiles to himself. "I thought my little girl could be like the girl in that book—Alicia in Wonderland! But I was wrong. My baby girl didn't see all the beauty—just the strangeness."

I feel like Trub's talking in riddles again. This time I ask for help. "Wait a minute. Are you saying you took Mama to another dimension when she was a little girl?"

Trub nods. "Just once, but once was all it took. She took a look around, shut her eyes as tight as she could, and demanded that I take her back home."

I can't wait to see the realm of magic—at least I'm curious about what it's like. It's hard to imagine my brave mother being so scared. But then I remember how terrified I was when Ma accidentally took me to the land of dinosaurs. If the magical realm has dragons, maybe Mama felt the same way.

Trub looks pretty miserable, so I try to think of something that will make him feel better. "Ma says Mama just wanted to be ordinary," I tell Trub.

He nods as if that makes sense to him. "Maybe so. What about you, Jax? What do you want?"

I think for a moment. Does Trub know that Mama and I are about to lose our home? Would he approve if I told him I wanted to become Ma's apprentice? I don't know the answers to those questions, so I just say, "I want to find Ma and make sure she's okay. And then I want to help her deliver the dragons."

Trub claps his hands together and gets up from the bench. "Then that's what we better do. You ready to go?"

I nod and hold Ma's purse close to my chest. It feels lighter than before, but then I remember what's missing. "I don't have Ma's compass," I tell Trub. "She had it on her when we got separated."

"That's good—she'll need it to find her way around," he says. Trub reaches into his pants pocket and pulls out a silver watch. "I got my own, so if you got the dragons, we're all set."

We're missing something else. I scan the street for a scruffy homeless man pushing an overflowing grocery cart. “Don’t we need Ambrose to open the door?” I ask.

Trub winks at me, and his gold tooth flashes between his smiling lips. “As it happens, picking locks is one of my specialties.”

10

I take a few steps toward the guardhouse and then realize Trub's heading in the opposite direction.

"Where are you going?" I call after him.

Trub crosses the cobblestone road that runs between the park's stone gateposts. "Let's use this one instead," he suggests. "We don't want to risk another unintended landing."

The park is closed to traffic, so I don't have to look both ways before I cross the road and follow Trub over to the other guardhouse. It's identical to the one Ma and I used last time. I watch as Trub pulls two thin metal rods from his shirt pocket. He sticks them into the lock in the center of the guardhouse door, and after a few twists of his wrist, the lock clicks open.

Trub pulls the door back and gestures for me to go inside. "After you, Jax."

I climb the two short steps but then turn and face my grandfather. "Where are we going, exactly?"

"I really can't say, Jax. The transporter reads our intentions, and we *intend* to find Ma—wherever she is."

"So . . . does that mean we're going back to the land of dinosaurs?" I ask in my bravest voice.

Trub shakes his head. "I doubt Ma would still be there. But I think she may be *in the vicinity,* so to speak. It's possible those dragons you got in that bag pulled the transporter off course—it read their intention instead of Ma's."

"And the dragons wanted to be with dinosaurs?"

"I guess they wanted to go home, but Ma had something else in mind, and you all landed in Gondwana instead."

"Gondwana? That's one of the supercontinents!"

Trub's eyebrows go up, and I can tell he's impressed. "That's right, son! How'd you hear about Gondwana?"

"Geography is one of my specialties," I tell him, though technically supercontinents fall under paleogeography. "The continents we know today were once merged. Gondwana eventually broke apart to form the continents in the Southern Hemisphere: Antarctica, Australia, South America, and Africa."

"Which includes Madagascar," Trub adds.

I think for a moment. "If that's where the dragons were born, then there must still be magic there."

Trub nods and says, "I expect so. Africa's called the cradle of civilization. Know why?"

"Sure," I reply. "That's where the human race started out."

"Right. And when humans began to migrate, they took magic with them all over the world."

"So what happened?"

Trub sighs and looks at the bustling avenue. We both wince as a fire truck races by with its lights flashing and sirens wailing. An ambulance follows close behind, and car horns blast as drivers try to get out of the way.

"That's a long story, Jax," Trub says in a weary voice. "Let's save it for another time."

"Okay," I say.

Trub nods toward the guardhouse. "You ready to go get Ma?"

I nod back at him and step inside the dark, musty guardhouse. Trub climbs in behind me and pulls the door shut. I hear him take a deep breath, so I do the same. Trub rests his hands on my shoulders and says, "Try to clear your mind, Jax. Focus on Ma and nothing else."

I do as I'm told and picture Ma in the jungle. She holds her cane in one hand and the sparkling crystal in the other. She isn't afraid, because she has magic on her side. It's pitch-black inside the guardhouse, but I see Ma's face clearly in my mind's eye. *We're coming, Ma,* I whisper. *We're coming back for you.*

Suddenly, the transporter shoots upward, making my full stomach heave. I clutch Ma's purse to my chest and focus on the picture of her in my mind. Trub's hands rest lightly on my shoulders, and I keep my knees loose so that I bounce like when I'm riding the bus in Brooklyn. The transporter dips and dives and then jerks to the left—hard.

"Did we just cross dimensions?" I ask Trub.

"We sure did," he says proudly. "Now brace yourself, Jax—we should land in just a few seconds."

My heart starts to race. What world will we step into this time?

The transporter shudders and then goes still. Just as I open my mouth to ask if we've arrived, the guardhouse plummets to the ground and lands with a thud.

Trub squeezes my shoulder. "You okay, Jax?" he asks.

I nod but then realize Trub needs to hear me say the words out loud. "I'm fine," I tell him—and I mean it. I'm nervous, but I'm not afraid.

Trub moves his hands from my shoulders to the door. He gives it a good shove, and the black iron door creaks open on stiff hinges. I don't think this transporter has been used in a while, but it seems to have brought us to the right destination. My racing heart slows as I take a deep breath and step out of the guardhouse.

I don't need Trub to tell me that we've landed in the realm of magic. This world is totally different from the land of dinosaurs I visited with Ma. The lavender sky above us shimmers with light even though I can't see the sun or the moon. The air is cool and dry, and butterflies twirl by on a gentle breeze. I take a deep breath and wonder if we're near the sea. I can't tell if the sun has just set or if it's about to rise, but everything in this world seems to be at peace.

The guardhouse has landed on a dirt road, and it stretches out before us like a never-ending carpet. On either side of the road are enormous, stately trees that look like their roots are growing into the sky instead of underground. Long turquoise grass moves in the breeze like gentle waves beneath the trees. They all seem to be a hundred feet tall, with no branches along their trunks except at the very top. The strange sheen on their bark makes me want to hug the tree closest to me, but my arms would never reach around its stout trunk. Even if Trub and Vik and Kavita held hands with me, we couldn't reach around any of these massive trees.

"So," Trub says after nudging me with his elbow, "what do you think?"

"It feels like we've landed on a whole other planet!" I exclaim as a blue butterfly tumbles by.

Trub laughs and takes a few steps down the road. "You coming?"

I nod and try to keep my mouth from falling open as I walk past the gigantic upside-down trees. I'm so excited I have to stop myself from skipping and turning cartwheels in the middle of the road. "Are we in Madagascar?" I ask.

"Not exactly," Trub replies. "Some . . . features of the world we live in are mirrored in the realm of magic. The beautiful ones, mostly."

"These trees—they're . . . so . . . so . . . I mean . . ." I finally stop trying to find the right word and just gaze up at the trees in awe. I don't know how to describe the way I feel. I'm the size of an ant compared to these trees, but I don't feel insignificant. If anything, being near these trees makes me feel important—safe—special.

Trub nods as if he understands what I'm trying to say. "In Madagascar, there's a place just like this, called the Avenue of the Baobabs. The Malagasy—the people who live in Madagascar—they call these trees renala. It means 'mother of the forest.' "

That makes perfect sense to me. Being near these magical trees makes me feel like I've got Mama's arms wrapped around me. But then I remember that Mama is actually far away, and that reminds me of our mission. "Where's Ma?" I ask Trub.

"She should be around here somewhere," Trub says as he scans the forest of baobabs.

"How did you know Ma would be here?" I ask.

"I didn't know for sure," Trub replies. "But when you showed me that book, I had a feeling Ma might find her way here."

"Is this where L. Roy Jenkins lives?" I ask, imagining what it would be like to live in such a magical place.

Trub shakes his head. "L. Roy doesn't really stay in one place—he's more of a nomad."

"A rolling stone?" I ask.

Trub nods. "I don't know if Ma told you this, Jax, but when it comes to the future of magic, there are two camps: those who feel the realms should remain separate, and those who want the realms to merge. Ma's in the first camp, and L. Roy's in the second. That's why he sent those dragons to Brooklyn. I expect he thought Ma would come around to his way of thinking on the matter."

"Which camp are you in?" I ask.

Trub takes a deep breath. "I really don't know, Jax. This realm is a sanctuary for many beings and creatures that just wouldn't be safe in our world. But the longer they stay hidden here, the more foreign and frightening they become to humans. People fear what they don't know, and when you're separated from folks just 'cause you're different . . . well, our people know what that feels like."

Trub's words feel like another riddle. I think maybe he's talking about segregation, when Black people were kept separate from Whites. It's not legal anymore, but I still have to take a bus to get to school because Mama didn't want me going to the school right around the corner from where we live. She said I'd learn more in an "integrated environment." I wonder what it would be like to live in a world integrated with magical creatures!

"Maybe we need a third camp," I suggest. "I mean, what if we could find a way to build a bridge between the two worlds? Then anyone who wanted to visit could cross over for a little while."

Trub places his hand on top of my head and gives my brain an approving squeeze. "That's just what we need, Jax—middle ground. See, that's why we need young folks like you on board. We need fresh ideas and a new way of looking at things. Us old folks are too stuck in our ways sometimes. And speaking of old folks, look who it is!"

11

I clutch Ma's purse and scan the horizon. Up ahead there's a bright orange tent with open flaps billowing in the breeze. Beneath it are three people—one is sitting on a stool, another is sitting on the ground, and a third is pacing back and forth. I search for Ma's snowy Afro, but it is vanishing between the fingers of the woman on the chair. Her own straight black hair is gathered in a single long braid, and her nimble brown fingers are weaving Ma's white hair into tidy cornrows.

Before I know what I'm doing, I burst into a sprint and race down the road. Trub's laughter floats in the air behind me, and all three people in the tent turn in my direction as a red cloud of dust rises at my heels. It's not easy to run when you have a heavy book bag on your back plus a purse in your hand, but I reach the tent in less than twenty seconds. I'm so happy to see Ma it feels like my heart will burst. But for some reason, I don't enter the tent. Instead, I just stand at the edge of the woven reed mat and stare at the three elders before me.

Ma is still wearing her purple housecoat. Her legs stretch out before her and are crossed at the ankles. Her black leather sneakers sit a few feet away, next to her carefully folded coat. On her lap is a cloth napkin, and in her hands Ma holds a knife and a large fruit that looks like the sun that's missing from the sky.

"Well, well, well—look who it is! You certainly took your time," Ma says with a wink.

I can only grin because I'm panting too hard to speak. With the knife, Ma peels the skin away to reveal flesh that is the same warm golden color. She slices off some fruit, but before eating it, Ma tilts her head to address the woman behind her. "I told you he'd figure out how to find me. The boy's smart as a whip!"

The woman nods but keeps her lips pressed together in a straight line. Her sharp eyes sweep over me, and I find myself blushing for some reason. A neon-green butterfly flits around her head before landing on her ear. It sits there for several seconds, opening and closing its wings, as if sharing a secret with the stern woman. Something tells me she's a witch, too, though she and Ma could just be related. Her skin is the color of coffee beans, and she has no wrinkles, though several silver strands are woven into her black braid.

The man has stopped pacing and stands with his hands clasped behind his back. He has a shiny brown bald head, glasses, and a white mustache that hides his mouth. He's wearing faded jeans with a hole in one knee and a brightly colored dashiki.

The green butterfly vanishes on the breeze when Trub reaches the tent. He immediately shakes hands with the man and says, "Nice to see you again, Professor."

"Always a pleasure, Trub," the man replies with a dignified bow.

"This is my grandson, Jaxon," Trub says with what sounds like pride.

"L. Roy Jenkins," the man announces before giving my hand a hearty shake. Then he takes off his round wire-framed glasses and peers into my face. "Strong family resemblance," he muses, as if I were a specimen in a science lab. "Does he share your . . . interest in magic? Or does he take after his mother?"

Before Trub can answer, Ma interrupts. "Jax is his own person, so don't you start comparing him to

anyone else. He's been a big help to me today. Jax, this here's Sis," Ma says, jabbing her thumb in the woman's direction.

"Nice to meet you, ma'am," I say, even though Sis doesn't seem that happy to meet me. She finishes the last braid and pats Ma's head as she admires her handiwork. Then she gathers up the tufts of white hair that are stuck in the teeth of her wooden comb. She rolls the hair into a ball and holds her palm up to her mouth. With one gentle puff, the ball of hair bursts into flame and vanishes.

I've never seen a woman who can breathe fire, but I try not to look shocked in case she takes offense.

Trub nods respectfully at Sis before stooping to kiss Ma on the cheek. "Sorry to keep you waiting, Ma," he says.

Trub steps back so I can greet Ma, but I still don't move—I can't. My feet that flew over the dirt road a moment ago now feel like lead. Ma sits on the mat calmly peeling the golden fruit. I want to throw my arms around her and squeeze her as tight as I can, but right now she seems harder to hug than the baobab trees.

Ma looks at me and frowns. "What's wrong, boy? Cat got your tongue? Here—have some of this."

Ma slices off a juicy wedge of fruit and passes it to me on the knife's blade. I take the slippery slice and shove it in my mouth. I savor the sweet fruit and then ask, "Mango?"

"What'd you think I was eating?" Ma replies with a spark of mischief in her eye.

I shrug and say, "Something magical, I guess."

"Can't improve on mangoes," Ma says. Then she nods at the bag I'm holding. "I see you brought my purse. Good work, Jax!"

I nod and proudly set it down beside her on the mat.

"Those dragons give you any trouble?" Ma asks.

I glance at Trub and say, "Well . . . just a little." Then I stick out my chest and add, "Nothing I couldn't handle."

Ma sets aside her mango and wipes her hands on the napkin. Then she opens her purse and takes out the red mint tin. She can tell right away that it's empty. "Where are they?" she asks anxiously.

"Uh, I had to move them to the side pocket," I say. I decide not to tell Ma why unless she asks.

Ma quickly unzips the side pocket and carefully takes out the sandwich bag. The dragons—bigger than the last time I saw them—strain against the plastic, whining pitifully. I beam with pride but eventually notice that no one else is smiling. In fact, everyone else looks worried. I peer more closely at the plastic bag and realize something *is* wrong—there are only *two* dragons in the bag!

Ma raises her eyes to meet mine. She's not angry—yet—but without meaning to, I've embarrassed Ma in front of her friends.

She takes a deep breath and says, "Jax, I've always tried to be honest with you, and now I need you to be honest with me. Did you lose the third dragon?"

"No!" I cry, blinking back tears of frustration.

Sis glares at me. "Did you think you could keep one for yourself?"

Stunned, I swallow hard and try to think of something to say. There were three dragons when I left Brooklyn, but there are only two in Ma's hand now!

I drop to my knees and rifle through Ma's purse. "They were there—all three of them! I put them in a sandwich bag, but the fire-breathing one melted the plastic, so I thought they'd be safer in that side pocket. . . ."

"I trusted you, Jax," Ma says with obvious disappointment.

Sis sucks her teeth and looks at me with disdain. "What did you expect from a mere *boy*?"

My face feels like it's on fire. "But . . ."

The dragon lady turns her full fury on the professor. "I trusted you, L. Roy. You swore you would keep my dragons safe."

"I kept my promise, Sis—your dragons have come to no harm. It's destiny!" L. Roy proclaims triumphantly. "Magic will find its way back into our world no matter how hard you try to keep it out, Ma."

"Actually," Trub says, "I think I know what happened to that last dragon. Nate did say he smelled a thief, and Jax has a little friend with sticky fingers. Right?"

I really don't want to solve another riddle right now, but as soon as Trub says "sticky," I know exactly what he means. "Kavita!" I shout angrily as if she could hear me. "She stole my dragon!"

"*My* dragon, you mean."

I look up to find Sis's laser-like eyes on me. The neon-green butterfly has been replaced with another. Its red wings beat so fast that it looks like a flame dancing around her stern face. I look down at Ma's empty purse to hide my shame.

Ma hands the two dragons over to Sis. As soon as she frees them from the plastic bag, they disappear in the folds of her shimmering dress. Ma closes her purse and clicks the latch. "Well," she says with a heavy sigh, "what do we do now?"

I jump up and volunteer, "I'll go back and get it, Ma! When Vik finds out what his sister's done, she'll be in so much trouble. . . ."

"Too late," L. Roy says with a smug smile on his face. "They're growing! This Kavita—she fed them, I presume?"

I avoid Ma's eyes again and nod reluctantly. L. Roy claps his hands and hops from one foot to the other.

“The remaining dragon will have grown attached to the girl already. I could have saved precious time and mailed them directly to *her* instead! Maybe that’s the way to ensure the future of magic—leave it to the kiddies!”

“Hush up, L. Roy,” Ma hisses. “I’m trying to think!”

For a moment, we all stand under the tent, waiting for Ma to come up with a solution. Finally, Trub clears his throat and says, “I’ll take the boy back to Brooklyn, Ma. We can pick up the last dragon and come straight back here.”

Ma shakes her head. “I appreciate the offer, Trub, but you don’t know what state that dragon is in now. It could be too big to transport if the girl’s been feeding it. And the other two dragons won’t thrive until they’re reunited with their sibling. No, this is something I need to handle myself.”

Ma holds out her hands, and Trub pulls her to her feet. L. Roy picks up Ma’s trench coat and holds it out as she slips her arms into the sleeves. I set Ma’s sneakers in front of her, and she slips them on without unfastening the Velcro straps. Sis hands Ma her cane.

“So much for retirement,” Ma says with a sigh. Then she pulls her purse straps over her shoulder and says, “Come on, Jax. Time to go home.”

I don't want to question Ma, but we can't all fit inside the transporter. Trub puts his hand on my shoulder and says, "I'm going to stay here with L. Roy, Jax. You go with Ma, and I'll catch up with you later."

My heart is already heavy, but now my throat starts to close, too. If Trub is a rolling stone, will I really see him again? I swallow hard and manage to squeak out one word. "Promise?"

Trub pulls me close and gives me a hug. "Promise. You are one brave boy, Jaxon! But you've done enough for one day. Go home and give that big brain of yours a rest. Us old folks will take it from here." Trub bends down and presses his lips to the top of my head. "Kiss your mama for me," he whispers in my ear before walking away from the tent.

L. Roy shakes my hand and looks at me over his glasses. "Remember, Jax," he says solemnly, "magic will find you—*if* you believe."

L. Roy turns and salutes Ma, who just rolls her eyes. Then he joins Trub, and together they head off down the red dirt road.

"I must make preparations for your journey," Sis says solemnly. She grabs hold of the wooden pole holding up the tent, and instantly everything around it disappears—the orange cloth, the stool, the reed mat, and the bowl of golden mangoes.

"I will wait for you at the gate," Sis tells Ma. She says nothing to me before wading into the blue grass growing beneath the baobab trees. I watch Sis walk away with the staff in her hands, wishing I had the courage to blurt out a promise—I *will* return your dragon! But before I build up the nerve, a sudden gust of wind blows dust into my eyes, and when I clear them, Sis has disappeared.

12

"Is Sis a witch?" I ask.

Ma shakes her head. "There are different roles here in the realm of magic. Sis is a guardian—and she takes her job very seriously. She isn't angry with you, by the way."

"Could've fooled me," I mumble.

"She's mad at herself for trusting us with something so precious. We all failed her, not just you."

That makes me feel a little bit better. I take a deep breath and say, "Ma, can I give you a hug?"

"Of course you can!" she cries before wrapping her arms around me.

I hold on tight for a long time. Then I step back and say, "I'm sorry about not delivering all the dragons, but I sure am glad you're okay."

Ma runs her thumb along my untamable eyebrows. "Why wouldn't I be?" Ma asks.

"You were attacked! I saw . . . something charging straight at you."

"What did you see?"

"Well . . ." I pause and try to remember just what I saw from inside the transporter. "The leaves behind you were shaking, and there was a load roar."

"And then?"

"Then you closed the door and the transporter took me back to Brooklyn."

I try to sound respectful, but Ma must hear the resentment in my voice because she says, "You understand why I did that, right?"

"You probably wanted to protect the dragons . . ." I say.

"And?"

I sigh. "And I guess you wanted to protect me, too. But I didn't want to go back to Brooklyn!"

"Sure you did—that's why the transporter sent you home. It reads your intention, remember?"

Ma starts walking down the road, and I trail after her. "But I was supposed to help you! I guess you don't want me to be your apprentice anymore," I say sullenly.

"When did I say that?" Ma barks angrily. "The first thing you got to learn if you're going to work with me, Jax, is how to follow orders. When I say go, you go! Understand?"

"Yes, ma'am."

"You did exactly what I needed you to do, and that helped a lot."

Even though I just got yelled at, I feel a smile tugging at the corners of my mouth. Maybe I haven't lost my dream job after all!

For a long while, we walk in silence. The baobab trees tower over us, and I start to feel their soothing energy settling over me. "Ambrose said you wouldn't have sent me back without a plan."

Ma laughs. "Did that make you feel better?"

I nod, and Ma says, "Then I'm glad Bro told you that. But the truth is, Jax, in this line of work, sometimes you don't have time to make a plan. Sometimes you just have to use whatever you've got to do whatever you can. Now, I'm not going to stand here and tell you I was happy to see that dinosaur coming straight at me. Ugly as sin it was, with more teeth than I could count."

My eyes grow wide as I imagine Ma having to face the most ferocious dinosaur of all. "A *T. rex*?"

"I doubt I'd be talking to you right now if a *T. rex* had popped out of the bushes! No, it was a lot smaller than that, but it walked the same way and had a funny kind of flap on top of its head."

I make a mental note to ask Vik what kind of dinosaur that might be. Then I ask, "So what did you do?"

"Why, I grabbed hold of that funny flap and swung around onto its back. Of course, that was after I'd zapped it a couple of times with my cane. Not sure it felt a thing with that thick hide, though. Then I used a mild enchantment to make it more manageable. Ran like the wind, that dinosaur!"

I wish I could have seen Ma riding on the back of an enchanted dinosaur! I don't know if it's the baobabs or Ma's story that makes me feel so happy, but I can't stop grinning. I may have lost one of the dragons, but I've got Ma back and we've got magic on our side.

Ma pats me on the shoulder and says, "That crystal you got for me came in real handy, Jax. I used it to send you back, and then I rode that dino as close as I could get to that volcano. All that energy helped me make a giant leap forward in time. Once I was back in the twenty-first century, I sent a signal to Sis. She gathered her lovelies—her helpers—and came to get me."

"But how could you travel through time without a transporter?"

"Same way I sent you back without me: piezo-electricity. Ever heard of that?"

I shake my head and listen carefully as Ma explains.

"The transporter is a device powered by the mind, and our brains give off electric signals. Well, crystals also give off an electric charge when they're under pressure. So I used a compression spell that allowed me to crush the crystal with my hand. That released enough energy to jump-start the transporter, and you steered it with your thoughts. When I was ready to make my own journey, I just needed a way to contain all the energy I was trying to harness—from my own mind, the crystal, and the volcano. So I found a hollowed-out tree, used my compass to set the right coordinates, and then . . . I got lucky."

I look ahead and see that Sis is waiting for us next to the guardhouse. At least a dozen butterflies circle her head and shoulders, wrapping her in a rainbow veil.

"The lost dragon must be returned to me," Sis says solemnly. "The girl is no thief—she now feels bound to the creature just as it feels bound to her. But those dragons—*all* of them—belong here, with me. They do not belong in your world."

"I know, Sis," Ma says. "And I sure am sorry things turned out this way. But we'll get this mess cleaned up—leave it with me."

Sis sweeps her dark eyes over me. "The boy cannot be trusted."

"Hold on, now," Ma says as she drapes a protective arm across my shoulders. "He's had a rough first day on the job, and Jax still has a lot to learn, but I trust him and I'll need his help to set things right."

"I will provide the help that you need," Sis says.

"That won't be necessary," Ma says with a smile that seems a bit forced.

"I insist," Sis replies in a way that makes it clear her offer cannot be refused.

Ma simply nods, and Sis raises her hand. The butterflies gather round, and Sis selects a fiery red one to accompany us back to Brooklyn. I watch as she cradles the butterfly in the palm of her hand, whispering instructions that Ma and I can't hear. The other butterflies wheel away on the breeze, and then the red one flits from Sis to me.

"Hold out your hand," Ma says.

I do as I'm told, and the red butterfly settles in my palm. I don't see how a flimsy butterfly is going to help us transport a fast-growing dragon, but Ma and Sis must know something I don't.

Sis runs her hand over Ma's neatly braided hair and says, "Remember your promise—when you return, you will stay."

For a moment Ma says nothing, and part of me

hopes she'll refuse. How will I learn all there is to know about magic if Ma retires so soon?

But after a few more seconds, Ma finally nods. Sis opens her arms, and Ma steps into a hug that lasts a long time. I look at the peaceful smile on Ma's face and wonder if that's how I look when Mama holds me. Finally, Ma and Sis pull apart. Ma goes over to the guardhouse and opens the door. I try to follow her, but Sis blocks my way.

"You have in your possession things that are precious to me. See that you treat them with care and return them unharmed, boy."

"My name's Jax," I tell her in my most respectful voice. "And I won't let you down, Sis." I'm not sure why, but I decide to add, "I promise."

One of Sis's eyebrows goes up in surprise. "A promise in this realm carries real weight, Jax."

"It means a lot in my world, too," I tell her.

Sis looks down at me, and I think I can see something in her eyes that wasn't there before: respect. She steps aside, and I squeeze past Ma to stand inside the dark guardhouse. To my surprise, the butterfly's red wings start to pulse with light as they slowly open and close. Maybe this little helper will come in handy after all.

"Until we meet again," I hear Sis say. Then the door closes, and Ma places her hands on my shoulders.

"Ready, Jax?" she asks.

"Ready, Ma," I reply.

The guardhouse shudders and then shoots upward and takes us back to Brooklyn.

13

When we land, Ma pushes open the guardhouse door. I follow the butterfly out and see that we're facing the street instead of the park. A bus lumbers along Flatbush Avenue, and the few joggers going in and out of the park barely notice me and Ma as we emerge from the guardhouse. I scan all the benches and feel a little disappointed when I don't find Ambrose. I want him to know that Trub and I completed our mission. I want him to see that Ma's okay. Part of me feels like I have to prove myself, especially since Ma's had trouble with her helpers in the past. I want Ambrose to know I'm not like the others. Once we collect the dragon from Kavita, everyone will know that I'm serious about being Ma's apprentice.

"Should we head over to Vik's place?" I ask Ma.

She glances up at the darkening sky and shakes her

head. "It's too late for a messy extraction—and it *will* be messy. We better think on it tonight and come up with a plan."

Ma opens her purse and takes out the mint tin. "In you go," she says to the red butterfly. I don't see how it will fit, but the butterfly perches on Ma's hand and instantly shrinks so that it can settle inside the small tin. "Just until we get home," Ma says.

She snaps the lid shut before tossing the tin back into her purse. Then Ma leans on her cane and heads up the block.

"Your mama must be wondering what happened to you."

I feel a pang of guilt as I think about what Mama's day must have been like. I traveled to the realm of magic while she was stuck in court. Did the judge rule in our favor, or are we homeless? I wonder what Mama will say when I tell her I want to work with Ma.

The streetlights flicker on as night settles over the noisy, bustling city. I miss the peace and calm of the baobabs and hope it won't be long before I get to see that world again. But if Ma goes back with me, she'll have to stay with Sis. Maybe Ma's plan to find the last dragon will take a long time. A "messy extraction" sounds like something painful that happens at the dentist's office. Even though I'm mad at Kavita for stealing the dragon, I hope no one gets hurt.

Ma doesn't say a word as we walk back to her apartment building. But when we reach her block, she clears her throat and asks, "You know what you're going to tell your mama 'bout today?"

I nod and say, "The truth."

I hope I sound confident, but Ma must know how nervous I am, because she gives my shoulder a squeeze. I give myself a pep talk the rest of the way: *Mama loves me. No matter what I say or do, that will never change.*

Mama is pacing back and forth in front of Ma's building. The clothes she ironed so carefully this morning are now rumpled, and her face shows how tired she feels. But when she sees us coming up the block, Mama rushes over, kneels down, and hugs me hard.

"Jaxon! Where have you been? I've been worried sick!" Mama pulls back and examines me from head to toe. She stands up and looks at Ma. "You need to get a cell phone."

Ma just laughs. "What for?"

I try to warn Ma with my eyes, but she's not looking at me. Mama hates it when people don't take her seriously. She puts one hand on her hip and says in a voice that's a bit too loud, "*What for?* So people can reach you, Ma! I didn't know what happened to you two. You could have left a note."

Ma glances at me and wipes the smile off her face. "Sorry 'bout that," she says in a sincere voice. "I didn't think we'd be gone so long, but things . . . didn't quite go as planned."

"They never do with you," Mama mutters under her breath.

I decide now's a good time to change the subject. "How did it go in court?" I ask Mama.

She smiles and strokes my cheek. "We got a stay, baby. That means the landlord can't go ahead with the eviction."

"So we can *stay* in our apartment?" I ask hopefully.

"For now," Mama says, "but I still have to go back to court next week."

"Well," Ma says, "I'm glad it all worked out. I better go see about supper."

"Wait!" I grab hold of Ma's hand to keep her from walking away. Then I reach out and grab hold of Mama's hand, too. This is my chance—I can be the bridge between them.

"Maybe we should stay with Ma for a while," I suggest.

Mama frowns and tries to pull away, but I won't let go of her hand.

"You can stay if you want," Mama tells me. "I need to keep an eye on the apartment."

"But there's no water," I remind her.

"No water?"

Ma looks kind of mad, so I tell her more about our awful landlord. "Last week he turned off the gas, too, so we couldn't cook."

Mama looks embarrassed. Maybe I said too much.

"We manage with the microwave," she tells Ma.

"You can't manage without running water," Ma replies. "You better come upstairs."

Mama doesn't budge. "The judge ordered the landlord to turn the water back on within forty-eight hours."

Ma just grunts. "Don't hold your breath." Then she coughs a couple of times before saying, "Listen, Alicia—I know I made a fuss this morning, and I'm sorry for that. You just caught me at a bad time. But I want you to know that you're always welcome here. You and Jax could stay in your old room—it hasn't changed since you left."

Mama squeezes my hand a little too hard and looks at the ground. Mama taught me everything I know about manners, so I know it's not polite to ignore an offer of hospitality.

Ma tries again. "I know things haven't been . . . right between us, but you'll always be family to me."

That reminds me of something I promised Trub. I pull at Mama's arm until she bends low enough so I can plant a kiss on her cheek. "Grandpa says hi," I say quietly.

Mama looks at me hard. "*Who* says hi?"

I swallow and force myself not to look at Ma. If I look at her, she'll think I need help, and I don't. I've already decided I'm not going to lie to Mama. I take a deep breath and say, "I met my grandfather today."

Mama rolls her lips together. That's what she does when she's trying not to lose her temper and say something she might regret. Mama's lips are sealed, but I can almost hear her counting to ten. That's what she tells me to do whenever I get angry.

Finally, she opens her mouth and asks, "How did that happen?"

Ma coughs softly, but I need to tell this story on my own. "I—I went with Ma to make a delivery today."

Mama quickly rolls and then unrolls her lips. I can tell she's angry but not with me. "You did, huh? That sounds interesting."

Mama's talking to me, but she's glaring at Ma. I try to get her eyes back on me.

"It was! But then we . . . we got separated and Trub—your father—he came to help me find Ma. And he took me out for a burger." Mama gives me a disapproving frown, so I add, "I like him. He's nice."

Mama rolls her eyes this time and says, "Never trust a first impression, Jax. It takes time to really get to know somebody."

"True," Ma says, "although sometimes you just got to go with your gut."

"Stay out of this, Ma."

I guess Ma doesn't hear the warning in Mama's voice because she says, "I'm just trying to tell the boy—"

Mama explodes. "I don't need you to tell my son anything! I left him with you for *ONE DAY,* and you've already got him mixed up in your—your—mess!"

Ma leans heavily on her cane, and for a moment I think she's going to walk away. But she doesn't. Instead, she leans forward so her face is just a few inches away from Mama's.

"You know what I am, Alicia. I'm a private person, but I don't believe in keeping secrets. I told Jax the truth. You should try it sometime."

Uh-oh. Mama's eyes flash with anger. "Don't you tell me how to raise my son."

Ma just shrugs. "I didn't come to you—you brought Jax to me."

"I had no choice!" Mama cries in exasperation.

"Sure you did," Ma says. "You could have taken him to court with you. But you chose to leave him with me. Whether you like it or not, things are going to be different from now on."

“What’s that supposed to mean?” Mama asks.

I tug her hand so that Mama looks at me instead of at Ma. “I’ve decided to become Ma’s apprentice,” I say with a mixture of fear and pride.

Mama blinks twice but says nothing at first. I force myself not to look away even when I see tears filling up my mother’s eyes.

“Oh, Jax,” Mama finally says with a sigh. Then she lets go of my hand and sinks onto the steps that lead up to Ma’s building.

Ma gently peels away my fingers from her hand and says, “I’m going to start supper. Come on up whenever you’re ready.”

As she climbs the stairs, Ma puts a hand on Mama’s shoulder, but Mama doesn’t respond. I watch Ma go inside her building, and then I take a seat next to my mother. Her fingers are laced together, and she holds them over her mouth like a net that will catch words she doesn’t want me to hear.

The tears in Mama’s eyes don’t fall. After a while, she puts her hands on her knees and asks, “Where did you go today, Jax?”

I try to use as few words as possible. “First, we went back in time—by accident. Then Trub took me to the realm of magic to find Ma. Then we came home.”

"He took me there once," Mama tells me in a strange, sad voice.

"I know," I say quietly. "Trub told me you didn't like it much."

Mama shakes her head and puts her arm around my shoulders so she can pull me close. "This world is the only one that matters, Jax. This is where you live. This is where you belong."

Mama's been through a lot today. It would be easier just to agree with her, but I try a different approach. "But . . . what if we could make this world better? Don't you think we should try?"

Mama thinks for a moment. Then she shifts on the stairs so that we're sitting face to face. "Magic won't bring your daddy back, Jax."

Mama's voice is so soft and low that at first I'm not sure I heard her correctly. But then my cheeks start to burn, and I feel hot tears filling up my eyes. Mama becomes a blur.

I blink a few times, and Mama comes back into focus. Her face is full of love, and that gives me the courage I need.

"I know that, Mama. Bad things happen, and sometimes there's nothing we can do. But this time, there *is* something I can do. I want to help Ma return the last dragon."

Mama's eyebrows shoot up. "Dragon? Oh, Jax . . ." Mama shakes her head slowly like there's no hope for me—like I'm lost to her already.

I rush on, trying to reassure her. "I can do it, Mama! And . . . I have to because . . . it's sort of my fault that the dragon is still stuck here in Brooklyn."

"You don't *have* to do anything, Jax," Mama says firmly. "Ma can handle her business without you. It's *her* job, not yours."

"I know," I tell Mama, "but . . . Ma's going to retire soon. So I need to do this now, Mama. Please?"

Mama doesn't say anything for what feels like a really long time. Then she scoots closer and puts her arm around me once more. "Why don't you tell me what it was like for you . . . in that other world?"

I open my mouth to say "Sure!" but suddenly my stomach growls—no, *roars*—with hunger.

Mama laughs and pokes me in the belly. "You got a dragon in there?" she asks with a smirk.

I laugh, too, and clutch my empty stomach. "Can I tell you about the dragons . . . and the dinosaurs . . . and the baobabs over supper?"

Mama kisses me on the forehead and says, “Sure.”

I take Mama’s hand, and together we go upstairs to join Ma.

ACKNOWLEDGMENTS

The "trouble" with magic, as it is represented in much of children's literature, is that it appears to exist in realms to which only certain children belong.

In 2012, while attending the Race, Ethnicity, and Publishing conference in Aix-en-Provence, France, I received an email inviting me to contribute to a scholarly anthology on urban children's literature. I'd never thought of myself as a traditional academic and planned to finish a fantasy novel in the coming months, so I declined; the anthology had been in production for over a year, and I suspected my last-minute invitation came only after the editors realized they hadn't included any scholars of color. They persisted, however, and eventually I agreed to write an essay about the need for inclusive fantasy fiction for youth.

I was frustrated—but not entirely surprised—

when the editors complained that my "tone" didn't fit with that of the other contributors to the anthology. I withdrew my essay from consideration and fumed for several weeks. Mostly I was angry at myself for wasting time writing a scholarly article when I knew my focus going forward would be fiction. Two years later, I quit my job as a professor in order to have more time to write, but first I dusted off my rejected essay and submitted it to an academic journal. Months after I left academia, "The Trouble with Magic: Conjuring the Past in New York City Parks" won the 2013 Article Award from the Children's Literature Association. I couldn't afford to fly to Virginia to accept the award, but I felt vindicated nonetheless.

Most of my manuscripts have been rejected by editors over the years, but I am slowly clearing my hard drive because I believe my writing deserves to exist in the world. I fully expected I would have to self-publish *Dragons in a Bag,* but my agent was able to find an editor who was open to this unconventional story. I'm grateful that Jennifer Laughran believed in me as a writer and wisely presented my book to Diane Landolf at Random House. In my article, I reflect on the books of another Brooklyn writer, Ruth Chew, and Diane happens to be a fan of Chew's work. Whether that's luck or fate, I don't know, but I couldn't have asked for a better editor. I would also like to thank Brooklyn Public Library youth librarian Yesha Naik for her help with selecting the right Gujarati dessert for my dragons, and Prof. Soniya Munshi for taking me to Maharaja Sweets. Geneva B's illustrations bring to life the magic of Brooklyn, and I'm thankful for her loving vision of my characters (#BlackGirlMagic, #BlackBoyJoy). My niece Portia was one of the first readers of this book, and I thank her for sharing her insights with me.

Writing a novel is, in some ways, like raising a child—it takes a village. I can't name everyone but want to thank all the members of my village for letting me dream, and write, and rant, and disappear when necessary.

Brooklyn is my heart. Like so many other residents, artists of color are being priced out of this beautiful borough, but I hope my book reminds us—as Jean Toomer once did—of what we have been and still can be:

. . . before they stripped the old tree bare
One plum was saved for me, one seed becomes

An everlasting song, a singing tree . . .